John Davies

The Poetical Works of Sir John Davies,

Consisting of his Poem on the Immortality of the Soul...

John Davies

The Poetical Works of Sir John Davies,
Consisting of his Poem on the Immortality of the Soul...

ISBN/EAN: 9783744764070

Printed in Europe, USA, Canada, Australia, Japan

Cover: Foto ©Andreas Hilbeck / pixelio.de

More available books at **www.hansebooks.com**

THE
POETICAL WORKS
OF
SIR JOHN DAVIES,

Confifting of his POEM on the

IMMORTALITY of the SOUL:
THE
HYMNS OF ASTREA;
AND
ORCHESTRA
A
POEM ON DANCING,
IN
A DIALOGUE

BETWEEN

PENELOPE and one of her WOOERS.

All publifhed from a correfted Copy,

Formerly in the Poffeffion of W. THOMPSON of
QUEEN'S COLL. OXON.

LONDON:
Printed for T. DAVIES, in Ruffel-Street, Covent-Garden.
M DCC LXXIII.

THE

PREFACE

TO

SIR JOHN DAVIES's POEM

ON THE

IMMORTALITY OF THE SOUL,

PUBLISHED IN 1699.

THERE is a natural love and fondnefs in En-glifhmen for whatever was done in the reign of Queen Elizabeth ; we look upon her time as our golden age ; and the great men who lived in it, as our chiefeft he-roes of virtue, and greateft examples of wifdom, cou-rage, integrity and learning.

a 2

Among

*Among many others, the author of this poem merits
a lasting honour ; for, as he was a most eloquent lawyer, so, in the composition of this piece, we admire him
for a good poet, and exact philosopher. 'Tis not rhyming
that makes a poet, but the true and impartial repre-
senting of virtue and vice, so as to instruct mankind
in matters of greatest importance. And this observation has been made of our countrymen, That Sir
John Suckling wrote in the most courtly and gentle-
man-like style ; Waller in the most sweet and flowing
numbers ; Denham with the most accurate judgment
and correctness ; Cowley with pleasing softness, and
plenty of imagination : none ever uttered more divine
thought than Mr. Herbert ; none more philosophical
than Sir John Davies. His thoughts are moulded
into easy and significant words ; his rhymes never
mislead the sense, but are led and governed by it :
so that in reading such useful performances, the wit
of mankind may be refined from its dross, their meme-
ries furnished with the best notions, their judgments
strengthened, and their conceptions enlarged, by which
means*

means the mind will be raised to the most perfect ideas it is capable of in this degenerate state.

  But as others have laboured to carry out our thoughts, and to entertain them with all manner of delights abroad; 'tis the peculiar character of this author, that he has taught us (with Antoninus) to meditate upon ourselves; that he has disclosed to us greater secrets at home; self-reflection being the only way to valuable and true knowledge, which consists in that rare science of a man's self, which the moral philosopher loses in a crowd of definitions, divisions and distinctions: the historian cannot find it amongst all his musty records, being far better acquainted with the transactions of a thousand years past, than with the present age, or with himself: the writer of fables and romances wanders from it, in following the delusions of a wild fancy, chimeras and fictions that do not only exceed the works, but also the possibility of nature. Whereas the resemblance of truth is the utmost limit of poetical liberty, which our author has very religi-

ously

ously observed; for he has not only placed and con-
nected together the most amiable images of all those
powers that are in our souls, but he has furnished
and squared his matter like a true philosopher; that
is, he has made both body and soul, colour and shd-
dow of his poem out of the store-house of his own mind,
which gives the whole work a real and natural
beauty; when that which is borrowed out of books,
(the boxes of counterfeit complexion) shews well or ill
as it has more or less likeness to the natural. But our
author is beholding to none but himself; and by knowing himself thoroughly, he has arrived to know much;
which appears in his admirable variety of well-chosen
metaphors and similitudes that cannot be found within
the compass of a narrow knowledge. For this reason
the poem, on account of its intrinsic worth, would be
as lasting as the Iliad, or the Æneid, if the language
'tis wrote in were as immutable as that of the Greeks
and Romans.

Note

Now it would be of great benefit to the beaus of our age to carry this glass in their pocket, whereby they might learn to think, rather than dress well: it would be of use also to the wits and virtuosos to carry this antidote about them against the poison they have sucked in from Lucretius or Hobbs. This would acquaint them with some principles of religion; for in old times the poets were their divines, and exercised a kind of spiritual authority amongst the people. Verse in those days was the sacred style, the style of oracles and laws. The vows and thanks of the people were recommended to their gods in songs and hymns. Why may they not retain this priviledge? for if prose should contend with verse, it would be upon unequal terms, and (as it were) on foot against the wings of Pegasus. With what delight are we touched in hearing the stories of Hercules, Achilles, Cyrus, and Æneas? Because in their characters we have wisdom, honour, fortitude, and justice, set before our eyes. It was Plato's opinion, that if a man could see virtue, he would be

strangely

strangely enamoured on her person. Which is the reason why Horace and Virgil have continued so long in reputation, because they have drawn her in all the charms of poetry. No man is so senseless of rational impressions, as not to be wonderfully affected with the pastorals of the ancients, when under the stories of wolves and sheep, they describe the misery of people under hard masters, and their happiness under good. So the bitter but wholesome Iambick was wont to make villainy blush; the Satire incited men to laugh at folly; the Comedian chastised the common errors of life; and the Tragedian made kings afraid to be tyrants, and tyrants to be their own tormentors.

Wherefore, as Sir Philip Sidney said of Chaucer, that he knew not which he should most wonder at, either that he in his dark time should see so distinctly, or that we in this clear age should go so stumblingly after him; so may we marvel at and bewail the low condition of poetry now, when in our plays scarce

any

any one rule of decorum is observed, but in the space of two hours and an half we pass through all the fits of Bedlam ; in one scene we are all in mirth, in the next we are sunk into sadness ; whilst even the most laboured parts are commonly starved for want of thought ; a confused heap of words, and empty sound of rhyme.

This very consideration should advance the esteem of the following poem, wherein are represented the various movements of the mind ; at which we are as much transported as with the most excellent scenes of passion in Shakespear, or Fletcher : for in this, as in a mirror (that will not flatter) we see how the soul arbitrates in the understanding upon the various reports of sense, and all the changes of imagination : how compliant the will is to her dictates, and obeys her as a queen does her king. At the same time acknowledging a subjection, and yet retaining a majesty. How the passions move at her command, like a well disciplined army ; from which regular

composure

composure of the faculties, all operating in their pro-
per time and place, there arises a complacency upon
the whole soul, that infinitely transcends all other
pleasures.

What deep philosophy is this! to discover the process
of God's art in fashioning the soul of man after his
own image ; by remarking how one part moves ano-
ther, and how those motions are varied by several
positions of each part, from the first springs and
plummets, to the very hand that points out the visible
and last effects. What eloquence and force of wit to
convey these profound speculations in the easiest lan-
guage, expressed in words so vulgarly received, that
they are understood by the meanest capacities.

For the poet takes care in every line to satisfy the
understandings of mankind : he follows step by step
the workings of the mind from the first strokes of
sense, then of fancy, afterwards of judgment, into
the

the principles both of natural and supernatural mo-
tives: hereby the soul is made intelligible, which
comprehends all things besides; the boundless tracks
of sea and land, and the vaster spaces of heaven;
that vital principle of action, which has always been
busied in enquiries abroad, is now made known to
itself; insomuch that we may find out what we
ourselves are, from whence we came, and whither
we must go; we may perceive what noble guests
those are, which we lodge in our bosoms, which are
nearer to us than all other things, and yet nothing
further from our acquaintance.

But here all the labyrinths and windings of the
human frame are laid open: 'tis seen by what pullies
and wheels the work is carried on, as plainly as if
a window were opened into our breast: for it is the
work of God alone to create a mind. — The next to
this is to shew how its operations are performed.

THE

hall; he was expelled the fociety of the Middle Temple. Upon this he retired to Oxford and profecuted his ftudies. Afterwards by the favour of Lord Ellemore, Keeper of the Great Seal, being reinftated in the Temple, he practifed the law as a barrifter; and was chofen a burgefs in the parliament held at Weftminfter 1601. Upon the death of Queen Elizabeth, our author went with Lord Hunfdon into Scotland to congratulate King James. That prince was learned himfelf, and a great encourager of learned men; when Hunfdon and his retinue were admitted into the king's prefence; his majefty enquired the names of the gentlemen who accompanied him; his lordfhip naming among the reft John Davies, the king prefently afked whether he was Nofce Teipfum, which was the title of his poem on the Immortality of the Soul, and being anfwered that he was, he gracioufly embraced him, and affured him of his favour. The king prefently after promoted him to the office of folicitor and then attorney general in Ireland, where in 1606 he was made ferjeant at law, and afterwards fpeaker of the houfe of commons in that kingdom; the year following he received the honour of knighthood from the king at Whitehall. In the year 1612 he publifhed a very valuable book,
called,

called, *A Discovery of the true Causes why Ireland was never entirely subdued, nor brought under Obedience of the Crown of England, until the Beginning of his Majesty's happy Reign.*

In this treatise, the author has proved that the old Irish had petitioned to be governed by the laws of England, and that that great blessing was denied them by the misrepresentations of interested and tyrannic men; who having obtained large grants of territory from the crown, oppressed in a most savage manner the ancient inhabitants as well as their own countrymen who were settled in Ireland. Great progress had been made by several able lord lieutenants, from Edward the Third's time to the end of Queen Elizabeth's reign, to redress many enormous grievances which this unhappy country had groaned under.

But the complete settlement of Ireland was re-reserved for James the First; and this is the great honour of his reign. He passed an act of oblivion to quiet the minds of the people, and established the English laws in every part of the kingdom. Judges were appointed to go the circuits regularly as in England: Sir Edward Pelham and Sir John
Davies

Davies were the firſt juſtices of aſſize that ever ſat in the counties of Tryrone and Tryconnell. By ſuch prudent regulations as theſe, the province of Ulſter, which had formerly been the ſeat of rebellion and diſtraction, was rendered the moſt peaceable and ſubmiſſive of any in the kingdom. The concluſion of this treatiſe is ſo much to the honour of the natives of Ireland, that I am ſure my reader will not be diſpleaſed with me for tranſcribing it.

" There is no nation of people under the ſun
" that doth love equal and indifferent juſtice better
" than the Iriſh, or will reſt better ſatisfied with
" the execution thereof, although it be againſt
" themſelves ; ſo as they may have the protection
" and benefit of the law, when upon juſt cauſe they
" do deſire it."

Sir John, in 1612 quitted the poſt of attorney-general in Ireland, and was made one of his majeſty's Engliſh ſerjeants at law. After his ſettling in England he was often appointed one of the judges of aſſize in the circuits. He married Eleanor Tonchet, youngeſt daughter of George Lord Audley, by whom he had a ſon an ideot, who died young, and a daughter named Lucy, married to
Ferdinand

Ferdinand Lord Haſtings, afterwards Earl of Huntingdon.

In 1626 Sir John was appointed Lord Chief Juſtice of the King's Bench; but before the ceremony of his inſtallation could be performed, he died ſuddenly of an apoplexy the 7th of December, at his houſe in the Strand, in the 57th year of his age. His lady was a woman of a ſingular character, and it is ſaid ſhe foretold her huſband's death; ſhe had, or pretended to have, the ſpirit of prophecy, and her predictions received from a voice which ſhe often heard were generally wrapped up in dark and obſcure expreſſions. It is commonly reported, that on the Sunday before Sir John's death, as ſhe was ſitting at dinner with him, ſhe ſuddenly burſt into tears; he aſking her the occaſion, ſhe anſwered, " Huſband, theſe are your funeral tears." To which he replied ; " Pray, therefore, ſpare your tears now, and I will be content you ſhall laugh when I am dead. In 1649 an account was publiſhed of this lady's ſtrange prophecies : She died in St. Bride's pariſh in London, the 5th of July, 1652, and was buried in St. Martin's church, near the remains of her huſband.

Sir John Davies, besides his Poems and his Account of the Reduction of Ireland before-mentioned, published reports and other books relating to the constitution and laws of this kingdom. Anthony Wood says, there were several of his manuscripts on various subjects, which were formerly in the library of Sir James Ware, and since that in the possession of Edward Earl of Clarendon; besides these which were chiefly of a political kind: the same author says there were also some epigrams written by Sir John, and a metaphrase of several of King David's Psalms, but never published. The Poem on the Soul, which he called Nosce Teipsum, was first published in 1599, and afterwards in 1622 with Hymns to Astrea in Acrostick verse; and Orchestra, a poem expressing the antiquity and excellence of dancing, in a dialogue between Penelope and one of her wooers, containing one hundred and thirty-one stanzas unfinished. Mr. W. Thompson, the author of a poem called Sickness, was a great admirer of our author: it is from a corrected copy that Sir John Davies's Poems are published: he observes in a note upon the acrosticks, that they are the only good things of that kind; and laments that the Poem on Dancing was left unfinished. Sir John, though a good lawyer and an eminent politician,

cian, was still more eminent as a scholar and a
poet. His poem on the Immortality of the Soul,
will make his name live as long as our language.

N. Tate republished this excellent work in 1699,
and introduced it with an admirable preface which
is here reprinted. The author of the Biographia
Britannia ascribes this preface to Tate, but it was
written in a style and manner superior to that writer's abilities; and Tate himself tells us that the
author was a clergyman whose name he was not
permitted to give the public.

I shall conclude this Life of Sir John Davies,
which is chiefly taken from Anthony Wood, with
the inscription on his monument, fixed on a pillar
near his grave:

" Vir, ingenio compto, rara facundia, oratione
" tum soluta tum numeris astricta feliciffimus : Ju-
" ridicam severitatem morum elegantia et amœni-
" ore eruditione mitigavit. Patronus fidus, judex
" incorruptus, ingenuæ pietatis amore, et anxiæ
" superstitionis contemptu juxta infigtis."

He was a man of fine abilities and uncommon eloquence, and a moſt excellent writer both in proſe and verſe. He tempered the ſeverity of the lawyer with the politeneſs and learning of the gentleman : he was a faithful advocate, an impartial judge ; and equally remarkable for a love of ſincere piety and a contempt of anxious ſuperſtition.

T H E

THE

A U T H O R's

D E D I C A T I O N

T O

QUEEN ELIZABETH.

To that clear majesty which in the North
  Doth, like another sun, in glory rise,
Which standeth fix'd, yet spreads her heav'nly worth;
  Loadstone to hearts, and loadstar to all eyes.

Like heav'n in all, like earth to this alone,
  That thro' great states by her support do stand;
Yet she herself supported is of none,
  But by the finger of th' Almighty's hand.

 To

To the divineſt and the richeſt mind,
   Both by art's purchaſe, and by nature's dow'r,
That ever was from heaven to earth confin'd,
   To ſhew the utmoſt of a creature's pow'r :

To that great ſpring, which doth great kingdoms
     move ;
   The ſacred ſpring, whence right and honour
    ſtreams,
Diſtilling virtue, ſhedding peace and love,
   In every place, as Cynthia ſheds her beams :

I offer up ſome ſparkles of that fire,
   Whereby we reaſon, live, and move and be,
Theſe ſparks by nature evermore aſpire,
   Which makes them now to ſuch a highneſs flee.

Fair ſoul, ſince to the faireſt body join'd,
   You give ſuch lively life, ſuch quick'ning pow'r ;
And influence of ſuch celeſtial kind,
   As keeps it ſtill in youth's immortal flower :

As

As where the fun is prefent all the year,
  And never doth retire his golden ray;
Needs muſt the fpring be everlaſting there,
  And every feafon like the month of May.

O ! many, many years may you remain
  A happy angel to this happy land :
Long, long may you on earth our emprefs reign,
  Ere you in heaven a glorious angel ſtand.

Stay long (ſweet fpirit) ere thou to heaven depart,
Who mak'ſt each place a heaven wherein thou art.

HER MAJESTY'S

            Devoted Subject

July 11,
  1592.
            And Servant,

        JOHN DAVIES.

                THE

THE

CONTENTS.

B.2

THE

CONTENTS.

Sect.

THE

THE
INTRODUCTION.

WHY did my parents send me to the schools,
 That I with *knowledge* might enrich my mind?
Since the *desire to know* first made men fools,
 And did corrupt the *root* of all mankind;

For when God's hand had written in the hearts
 Of the first parents, all the rules of good,
So that their skill infus'd, did pass all arts
 That ever were, before, or since the flood;

---

* This poem was published by Mr. *Tate* with the universal applause of the nation; and was without dispute, except *Spencer's* Fairy Queen, the best that was written in Queen *Elizabeth's*, or even King *James* the First's time.

W. B.

And when their reasons eye was sharp and clear,
   And (as an eagle can behold the sun)
Could have approach'd th' eternal light as near,
   As th' intellectual angels could have done:

E'en then to them th' *spirit of lies* suggests,
   That they were blind, because they saw not *ill*,
And breath'd into their incorrupted breasts
   A curious *wish*, which did corrupt their *will*.

For that same ill they straight desir'd to know;
   Which ill, being naught but a defect of good,
In all God's works the Devil could not show,
   While man their Lord in his perfection stood.

So that themselves were first to *do* the ill,
   Ere they thereof the knowledge could attain,
Like him that knew not poison's power to kill,
   Until (by tasting it) himself was slain.

E'en so by tasting of that fruit forbid,
   Where they sought *knowledge,* they did *error* find;
Ill they desir'd to know, and ill they did;
   And to give *passion* eyes, made *reason* blind.

                             For

For then their minds did firſt in *paſſion* ſee
 Thoſe wretched ſhapes of *miſery* and *woe*,
Of *nakedneſs*, of *ſhame*, of *poverty*,
 Which then their own *experience* made them know.

But then grew *reaſon* dark, that *ſhe* no more,
 Could the fair forms of *good* and *truth* diſcern,
Bats they became, that *eagles* were before ;
 And this they got by their *deſire to learn*.

But we, their wretched offspring, what do we ?
 Do not we ſtill taſte of the fruit forbid ?
Whilſt with fond fruitleſs curioſity,
 In books profane we ſeek for knowledge hid.

What is this *knowledge ?* but the ſky-ſtol'n fire,
 For which the *thief* * ſtill chain'd in ice doth ſit ?
And which the poor rude *ſatyr* † did admire,
 And needs would kiſs, but burnt his lips with it.

---

* Prometheus.   † See Æſop's Fables.

What is it ?, but the cloud of empty rain,
  Which when *Jove's guest* * embrac'd, he monsters
    got ?
Or the false *pails*, † which oft being fill'd with pain ?
  Receiv'd the water, but retain'd it not ?

In fine, what is it ? but the fiery coach
  Which the *youth* ‡ sought, and sought his death
    withal ?
Or the *boy's* § wings, which when he did approach
  The *sun's* hot beams, did melt and let him fall ?

And yet alas ! when all our lamps are burn'd,
  Our Bodies wasted, and our spirits spent ;
When we have all the learned *volumes* turn'd
  Which yield men's wits both help and ornament :

What can we know ? or what can we discern ?
  When *error* choaks the windows of the mind ;
The divers forms of things, how can we learn ?
  That have been ever from our birth-day blind ?

---

* Ixion.   † Danaides.   ‡ Phaeton.   § Icarus.

When

When *reafon's* lamp, which (like the *fun* in fky)
    Throughout *man's* little world her beams did fpread,
Is now become a fparkle, which doth lie
    Under the afhes, half extinct, and dead:

How can we hope, that through the eye and ear,
    This dying fparkle, in this cloudy place,
Can recollect thefe beams of knowledge clear,
    Which were infus'd in the firft minds by grace?

So might the heir, whofe father hath in play
    Wafted a thoufand pounds of ancient rent,
By painful earning of one groat a·day,
    Hope to reftore the patrimony fpent.

The wits that div'd moft deep, and foar'd moft high.
    Seeking man's pow'rs, have found his weaknefs fuch:
" Skill comes fo flow, and life fo faft doth fly,
    " We learn fo little and forget fo much."

For this the wifeft of all moral men
    Said, *He knew nought, but that he nought did know,*
And the great mocking-mafter mock'd not then,
    When he faid, *Truth was buried deep below.*

For how may we to other things attain,
  When none of us his own *Soul* underſtands ?
For which the Devil mocks our curious brain,
  When, *know thyſelf*, his oracle commands.

For why ſhould we the buſy *Soul* believe,
  When boldly ſhe concludes of that and this,
When of herſelf ſhe can no judgment give,
  Nor how, nor whence, nor where, not what ſhe is,

All things without, which round about we ſee,
  We ſeek to know, and how therewith to do :
But that whereby we *reaſon, live and be,*
  Within ourſelves, we ſtrangers are thereto.

We ſeek to know the moving of each ſphere,
  And the ſtrange cauſe of th' ebbs and floods of *Nile* ;
But of that *clock* within our breaſts we bear,
  The ſubtle motions we forget the while.

We that acquaint ourſelves with ev'ry *zone*,
  And paſs both *tropicks*, and behold each *pole*,
When we come home, are to ourſelves unknown,.
  And unacquainted ſtill with our own *Soul.*

We

We ſtudy *ſpeech* but others we perſuade,
   We *leech-craft* learn, but others cure with it,
We interpret *laws*, which other men have made,
   But read not thoſe which in our hearts are writ.

Is it becauſe the mind is like the eye,
   Through which it gathers knowledge by degrees,
Whoſe rays reflect not, but ſpread outwardly ;
   Not ſeeing itſelf, when other things it ſees ?

No, doubtleſs ; for the mind can backward caſt
   Upon herſelf, her underſtanding's light,
But ſhe is ſo corrupt, and ſo defac'd,
   As her own image doth herſelf affright.

As is the Fable of the Lady fair,
   Which for her luſt was turn'd into a cow,
When thirſty to a ſtream ſhe did repair,
   And ſaw herſelf transform'd ſhe wiſt not how :

At firſt ſhe ſtartles, then ſhe ſtands amaz'd ;
   At laſt with terror ſhe from thence doth fly,
And loathes the wat'ry glaſs wherein ſhe gaz'd,
   And ſhuns it ſtill, though ſhe for thirſt doth die :

E'en

Neither *Minerva*, nor the learned *Muſe*,
   Nor rules of *art*, nor *precepts* of the wiſe,
Could in my brain thoſe beams of ſkill infuſe,
   As but the glance of this *dame's* angry eyes.

She within *Liſts* my ranging mind hath brought,
   That now beyond myſelf I will not go ;
Myſelf am *centre* of my circling thought,
   Only *myſelf* I ſtudy, learn, and know.

I know my Body's of ſo frail a kind,
   As force without, fevers within can kill :
I know the heavenly nature of my mind,
   But 'tis corrupted both in *wit* and *will*:

I know my *Soul* hath power to know all things,
   Yet is ſhe blind and ignorant in all :
I know I'm one of *nature's* little kings,
   Yet to the leaſt and vileſt things am thrall.

I know my life's a *pain*, and but a *ſpan*,
   I know my *ſenſe* is mock'd in ev'ry thing,
And to conclude, I know myſelf a man,
   Which is a *proud*, and yet a *wretched* thing.

OF THE

SOUL OF MAN,

AND THE

Immortality thereof.

*T*HE *lights of heav'n* (which are the world's fair
   eyes)
   Look down into the world, the world to see;
And as they turn, or wander in the skies,
   Survey all things, that on this centre be.

And yet the *lights* which in my *tow'r* do shine,
   Mine *eyes* which view all objects, nigh and far,
Look not into this little world of mine,
   Nor see my face, wherein they fixed are.

Since

Since *nature* fails us in no needful thing,
   Why want I means my inward self to fee ?
Which fight the knowledge of myfelf might bring,
   Which to true wifdom is the firft degree.

That *pow'r,* which gave me eyes the world to view,
   To view myfelf, infus'd an *inward light,*
Whereby my *Soul,* as by a *mirror true,*
   Of her own *form* may take a perfect fight.

But as the fharpeft *eye* difcerneth nought,
   Except the *fun-*beams in the air do fhine :
So the beft *Scul,* with her reflecting thought,
   Sees not herfelf without fome light divine.

O *light* which mak'ft the light, which makes the day !
   Whilh fet'ft the eye without, and mind within ;
'Lighten my fpirit with one clear heavenly ray,
   Which now to view itfelf doth firft begin.

For her true form how can my fpark difcern,
   Which dim by *nature, art* did never clear ?
When the great wits, of whom all fkill we learn,
   Are ignorant both *what* fhe is, and *where.*

One

One thinks the *Soul* is air; another, *fire*;
 Another *blood*, diffus'd about the heart;
Another faith, the *elements* conspire,
 And to her *essence* each doth give a part.

Musicians think our *Souls* are *harmonies*,
 Physicians hold that they *complexions* be;
Epicures make them swarms of *atomies*,
 Which do by chance into our Bodies flee.

Some think one gen'ral *Soul* fills ev'ry brain,
 As the bright *sun* sheds light in every star;
And others think the name of *Soul* is vain,
 And that we only *well-mixt* Bodies are.

In judgment of her *substance* thus they vary,
 And thus they vary in judgment of her *seat*;
For some her chair up to the brain do carry,
 Some thrust it down into the *stomach's* heat.

Some place it in the root of life, the *heart*;
 Some in the *river*, fountain of the veins,
Some say, *she's all in all*, and *all in ev'ry part*:
 Some say, she's not contain'd, but all contains.

Thus

Thus thefe great clerks their little wifdom fhow,
  While with their doctrines they at *hazard* play ;
Toffing their light opinions to and fro,
  To mock the *lewd,* as learn'd in this as they.

For no craz'd brain could ever yet propound,
  Touching the *Soul,* fo vain and fond a thought ;
But fome among thefe mafters have been found,
  Which in their *fchools* the felf-fame thing have
      taught.

God only wife, to punifh pride of wit,
  Among men's wits hath this confufion wrought,
As the proud *tow'r* whofe points the clouds did hit,
  By tongues confufion was to ruin brought.

But *(thou)* which didft *man's foul* of nothing make,
  And when to nothing it was fallen again,
  " To make it new, the form of man didft take ;
    " And *God* with *God,* becam'ft a *man* with men."

Thou that haft fafhion'd twice this *Soul* of ours,
  So that fhe is by double title thine,
Thou only know'ft her nature and her pow'rs ;
  Her fubtil form thou only canft define.

To

To judge herself, she must herself transcend,
 As greater circles comprehend the less:
But she wants pow'r, her own pow'rs to extend,
 As fetter'd men cannot their strength express.

But thou bright *morning-star*, thou *rising-sun*,
 Which in these later times hast brought to light
Those mysteries, that, since the world begun,
 Lay hid in darkness, and eternal night.

Thou *(like the sun)* do'st with an equal ray,
 Into the *palace* and the *cottage* shine,
And shew'st the *Soul*, both to the clerk and lay,
 By the clear *lamp* of *oracle* divine.

This lamp, through all the regions of my brain,
 Where my *Soul* sits, doth spread such beams of grace,
As now, methinks, I do distinguish plain,
 Each subtle line of her *immortal* face.

The Soul a substance, and a *spirit* is,
 Which *God* himself doth in the Body make,
Which makes the *man*, for every man from this,
 The *nature* of a *man*, and *name* doth take.

       And

And though this spirit be to th' Body knit,

   As an apt means her pow'rs to exercise,

Which are *life*, *motion*, *sense*, and *will*, and *wit*,

   Yet she *survives*, although the Body *dies*.

SECT. I.

That the SOUL *is a Thing subsisting by itself*
      without the Body.

S HE *is a* *substance*, and *a real* thing,

   Which hath itself an actual working might,

Which neither from the *senses* power doth spring,

   Nor from the *Body's humours* temper'd right.

She is a *vine*, which doth no propping need

   To make her spread herself, or spring upright;

She is a *star*, whose beams do not proceed

   From any *sun*, but from a *native* light.

                                     For

For when she forts things *prefent* with things *paft*,
   And thereby things to *come* doth oft forefee;
When she doth *doubt* at firft, and *chufe* at laft,
   Thefe acts her *own*, * without her Body be.

When of the dew, which th' *eye* and *ear* do take
   From flow'rs abroad, and bring into the brain,
She doth within both wax and honey make :
   This work is her's, this is her proper pain.

When she from fundry acts, one fkill doth draw;
   Gathering from divers fights one art of war;
From many cafes, like one rule of law;
   Thefe her collections, not the *fenfes* are.

When in th' *effects* she doth the *caufes* know,
   And feeing the ftream, thinks where the fpring doth
     rife;
And feeing the branch, conceives the root below;
   Thefe things she views without the Body's eyes.

---

* That the *Soul* hath a proper operation without the Body.

When she, without a *Pegafus*, doth fly
   Swifter than lightning's fire from *Eaſt to Weſt* ;
About the *centre*, and above the *fky*,
   She travels then, although the Body reſt.

When all her works ſhe formeth firſt within,
   Proportions them, and ſees their perfect end ;
Ere ſhe in act doth any part begin,
   What inſtruments doth then the Body lend ?

When without hands ſhe doth thus *caſtles* build,
   Sees without eyes, and without feet doth run ;
When ſhe digeſts the world, yet is not fill'd ;
   By her own *pow'rs* theſe miracles are done.

When ſhe defines, argues, divides, compounds,
   Conſiders *virtue*, *vice*, and *general things* ;
And marrying divers principles and grounds,
   Out of their match a true concluſion brings.

Theſe actions in her cloſet, all alone,
   (Retir'd within herſelf) ſhe doth fulfil ;
Uſe of her Body's organs ſhe hath none,
   When ſhe doth uſe the pow'rs of wit and will.

                                Yet

Yet in the Body's prison so she lies,
   As through the Body's windows she must look,
Her divers powers of *sense to exercise.*
   By gath'ring notes out of the *world's* great book.

Nor can herself discourse or judge of ought,
   But what the *sense* collects, and home doth bring;
And yet the pow'rs of her discoursing thought,
   From these collections is a *diverse* thing.

For though our eyes can nought but colours see,
   Yet colours give them not their pow'r of sight:
So, though these fruits of *sense* her objects be,
   Yet she discerns them by her proper light.

The workman on his stuff his skill doth show,
   And yet the stuff gives not the man his skill:
Kings their affairs do by their servants know,
   But order them by their own royal will.

So, though this cunning mistress, and this queen,
   Doth, as her instruments, the *senses* use,
To know all things that are *felt, heard,* or *seen;*
   Yet she herself doth only *judge* and *chuse.*

E'en as a prudent *emperor*, that reigns
 By *sovereign* title over sundry lands,
Borrows, in mean affairs, his subjects pains,
 Sees by their eyes, and writeth by their hands:

But things of weight and confequence indeed,
 Himfelf doth in his chamber them debate;
Where all his counfellors he doth exceed,
 As far in judgment, as he doth in state.

Or as the man whom *princes* do advance,
 Upon their gracious *mercy-feat* to fit,
Doth common things, of courfe and circumftance,
 To the *reports* of common men commit:

But when the caufe itfelf muft be decreed,
 Himfelf in perfon, in his proper court,
To grave and folemn hearing doth proceed,
 Of ev'ry proof, and ev'ry bye-report.

Then, like God's angel, he pronounceth right,
 And milk and honey from his tongue doth flow:
Happy are they that ftill are in his fight,
 To reap the wifdom which his lips do fow.

Right

Right fo the *Soul*, which is a lady free,
 And doth the juftice of her *ftate* maintain :
Becaufe the fenfes ready fervants be,
 Attending nigh about her court, the brain :

By them the forms of outward things fhe learns,
 For they return into the *fantafie*,
Whatever each of them abroad difcerns ;
 And there enroll it for the mind to fee.

But when fhe fits to judge the *good* and *ill*,
 And to difcern betwixt the *falfe* and *true*,
She is not guided by the *fenfes* fkill,
 But doth each thing in her own *mirror* view.

Then fhe the *fenfes* checks, which oft do err,
 And e'en againft their falfe *reports* decrees ;
And oft fhe doth condemn what they prefer ;
 For with a pow'r above the *fenfe*, fhe fees.

Therefore no *fenfe* the precious joys conceives,
 Which in her private contemplations be ;
For then the ravifh'd fpirit th' *fenfes* leaves,
 Hath her own pow'rs, and proper actions free.

C 3

Her

Her harmonies are sweet, and full of skill,
    When on the Body's instruments she plays;
But the proportions of the *wit* and *will*,
    Those sweet accords are even th' angels lays.

These tunes of *reason* are *Amphion's* lyre,
    Wherewith he did the *Theban* city found:
These are the notes wherewith the heavenly *choir,*
    The praise of him which made the heav'n doth
    found.

Then her *self-being nature* shines in this,
    That she performs her *noblest* works *alone :*
" The *work,* the touch-stone of the *nature* is;
    " And by their *operations,* things are known."

S E C T.

S E C T. II.

That the SOUL is more than a Perfection, or Reflection of the Sense.

A R E they not senseless then, that think the *Soul*
  Nought but a fine perfection of the *Sense,*
Or of the forms which *fancy* doth enroll;
  A *quick resulting,* and a *consequence ?*

What is it then that doth the *Sense* accuse,
  Both of *false judgment,* and *fond appetites ?*
What makes us do what *Sense* doth most refuse,
  Which oft in torment of the *Sense* delights ?

Sense thinks the *planets spheres* not much asunder :
  What tells us then their distance is so far ?
Sense thinks the lightning born before the thunder :
  What tells us then they both together are ?

When men seem crows far off upon a tow'r,
  Sense saith, they're crows : What makes us think
    them men ?
When we in *agues,* think all sweet things sour,
  What makes us know our tongue's false judgment
    then ?

What

What pow'r was that, whereby *Medea* saw,
　　And well approv'd, and prais'd the better courſe ;
When her rebellious *Senſe* did ſo withdraw
　　Her feeble pow'rs, that ſhe purſu'd the worſe ?

Did *Senſe* perſuade *Ulyſſes* not to hear
　　The mermaid's ſongs which ſo his men did pleaſe,
That they were all perſuaded, through the ear,
　　To quit the ſhip and leap into the *ſeas ?*

Could any pow'r of *Senſe* the *Roman* move,
　　To burn his own right-hand with courage ſtout ?
Could *Senſe* make *Marius* ſit unbound, and prove
　　The cruel lancing of the knotty gout ?

Doubtleſs, in *man* there is a *nature* found,
　　Beſide the *Senſes* and above them far ;
" Tho' moſt men being in ſenſual pleaſures drown'd,
　　" It ſeems their *Souls* but in their *Senſes* are."

If we had nought but *Senſe*, then only they
　　Should have found minds, which have their *Senſes*
　　　　found :
But *wiſdom* grows, when *Senſes* do decay ;
　　And *folly* moſt in quickeſt *Senſe* is found.

If

If we had nought but *Sense*, each living wight,
   Which we call *brute*, would be more sharp than we;
As having *Sense's apprehensive might*,
   In a more clear and excellent degree.

But they do want that *quick discoursing pow'r*,
   Which doth in us the erring *sense* correct;
Therefore the *bee* did suck the painted flow'r,
   And *birds*, of grapes, the cunning shadow peck'd.

Sense outsides knows, the *Soul* thro' all things sees:
   Sense, *circumstance*; she doth the *substance* view:
Sense sees the bark; but she the life of trees:
   Sense hears the sounds; but she the concords true.

But why do I the *Soul* and *Sense* divide,
   When *Sense* is but a *pow'r*, which she extends;
Which being in divers parts *diversify'd*,
   The divers *forms* of objects apprehends?

This power spreads outward, but the *root* doth grow
   In th' inward *Soul*, which only doth perceive;
For th' *eyes* and *ears* no more their objects know,
   Than *glasses* know what faces they receive.

For if we chance to fix our thoughts elsewhere,
　　Though our eyes open be, we cannot fee :
And if one *pow'r* did not both fee and hear,
　　Our fights and founds would always double be.

Then is the *Soul* a nature, which contains
　　The pow'r of *Senfe*, within a greater pow'r ;
Which doth employ and ufe the *Senfe*'s pains,
　　But fits and rules within her private bow'r.

SECT. III.

That the SOUL *is more than the Temperature
of the Humours of the Body.*

IF *fhe doth then* the fubtle *fenfe* excel,
　　How grofs are they that drown her in the blood ?
Or in the Body's humours temper'd well ;
　　As if in them fuch high perfection ftood ?

　　　　　　　　　　　　　　　　　As

As if most skill in that *musician* were,
  Which had the best, and best tun'd *instrument* ?
As if the *pencil* neat, and *colours* clear,
  Had pow'r to make the *painter* excellent ?

Why doth not *beauty* then refine the *wit*,
  And good complexion rectify the *will* ?
Why doth not *health* bring *wisdom* still with it ?
  Why doth not sickness make men brutish still.

Who can in *memory*, or *wit*, or *will*,
  Or *air*, or *fire*, or *earth*, or *water* find ?
What alchymist can draw, with all his skill,
  The *quintessence* of these out of the mind ?

If th'*elements* which have nor *life*, nor *sense*,
  Can breed in us so great a *pow'r* as this,
Why give they not *themselves* like excellence,
  Or other things wherein their *mixture* is ?

If she were but the Body's quality,
  Then she would be with it *sick*, *maim'd* and *blind*:
But we perceive where these privations be,
  An *healthy*, *perfect*, and *sharp-sighted* mind.

If

If she the Body's nature did partake,
  Her strength would with the Body's strength *decay:*
But when the Body's strongest sinews slake,
  Then is the *Soul* most active, quick and gay.

If she were but the Body's accident,
  And her sole being did in it subsist,
As *white in snow,* she might herself absent,
  And in the Body's substance not be miss'd.

But *it* on *her,* not *she* on *it* depends;
  For *she* the Body doth sustain and cherish:
Such secret pow'rs of life to it she lends,
  That when they fail, then doth the Body perish.

Since then the *Soul works by herself alone,*
  Springs not from Sense, nor *humours well agreeing,*
Her nature is peculiar, and her own;
  She is a *substance,* and a *perfect being.*

SECT.

S E C T. IV.

That the Soul is a Spirit.

*B*UT though this fubftance be the root of *fenfe*,
  Senfe knows her not, which doth but *Bodies* know:
She is a Spirit, and heav'nly influence,
  Which from th' fountain of God's fpirit doth flow.

She is a *Spirit*, yet not like *air*, or *wind*;
  Nor like the *fpirits* about the *heart*, or *brain* ;
Nor like thofe fpirits which alchymifts do find,
  When they in ev'ry thing feek gold in *vain*.

For fhe all *natures* under heav'n doth pafs,   [fee,
  Being like thofe fpirits, which God's bright face do
Or like *Himfelf*, whofe *image* once fhe was,
  Though now (alas!) fhe fcarce his *fhadow* be.

For of all *forms*, fhe holds the firft degree,
  That are to grofs, material bodies knit;
Yet fhe herfelf is *bodylefs*, and free;
  And though confin'd, is almoft infinite.

Where

Were she a *Body*, * how could she remain
   Within this Body, which is *less* than she?
Or how could she the world's great shape contain,
   And in our narrow breasts contained be?

All *Bodies* are confin'd within some place,
   But *she* all place within herself confines:
All *Bodies* have their measure and their space;
   But who can draw the *Soul*'s dimensive lines?

No *Body* can at once two forms admit,
   Except the one the other do deface;
But in the *Soul* ten thousand forms do sit,
   And none intrudes into her neighbour's place.

All *Bodies* are with other *Bodies* fill'd,
   But she receives both *heav'n* and *earth* together:
Nor are their forms by rash encounter spill'd,
   For there they stand, and neither toucheth either.

---

* That it cannot be a Body.

Nor

Nor can her wide embracements filled be;
  For they that most and greatest things embrace,
Enlarge thereby their mind's capacity,
  As streams enlarg'd, enlarge the channel's space.

All things receiv'd, do such proportion take,
  As those things have, wherein they are receiv'd:
So little glasses little faces make,
  And narrow webs on narrow frames are weav'd.

Then what vast Body must we make the *mind,*
  Wherein are men, beasts, trees, towns, seas and lands;
And yet each thing a proper place doth find,
  And each thing in the true *proportion* stands?

Doubtless, this could not be, but that she turns
  Bodies to Spirits, by *sublimation* strange;
As fire converts to fire the things it burns;
  As we our meats into our nature change.

From their gross *matter* she abstracts the *forms,*
  And draws a kind of *quintessence* from things;
Which to her proper nature she transforms,
  To bear them light on her celestial wings.

                            This

This doth she, when, from things *particular*,
  She doth abstract the *universal kinds*,
Which bodyless and immaterial are,
  And can be only lodg'd within our minds.

And thus from divers *accidents* and *acts*,
  Which do within her observation fall,
She goddesses, and pow'rs divine abstracts;
  As *nature*, *fortune*, and the *virtues* all.

Again; how can she sev'ral *Bodies* know,
  If in herself a *Body*'s form she bear?
How can a mirror sundry faces show,
  If from all shapes and forms it be not clear?

Nor could we by our eyes all colours learn,
  Except our eyes were of all colours void;
Nor sundry tastes can any tongue discern,
  Which is with gross and bitter humours cloy'd.

Nor can a man of *passions* judge aright,
  Except his mind be from all passions free:
Nor can a *judge* his office well acquit,
  If he possess'd of either party be.

If, laftly, this quick pow'r a Body were,
   Were it as fwift as is the wind or fire,
(Whofe *atoms* do the one down fide-ways bear,
   And th' other make in *pyramids* afpire.)

Her nimble Body yet in time muft move,
   And not in inftants thro' all places flide:
But fhe is nigh and far, beneath, above,
   In point of time, which thought cannot divide:

She's fent as foon to *China*, as to *Spain*;
   And thence returns, as foon as fhe is fent:
She meafures with one time, and with one pain,
   An ell of filk, and heav'ns wide fpreading tent.

As then the *Soul* a fubftance hath alone,
   Befides the Body in which fhe's confin'd;
So hath fhe not a Body of her own,
   But is a *fpirit*, and *immaterial mind*.

Since Body and Soul have fuch diverfities,
   Well might we mufe, how firft their *match* began;
But that we learn, that *he* that fpread the fkies,
   And fix'd the earth, firft form'd the *Soul* in man.

This

This true, *Prometheus* firſt made man of earth,
　And ſhed in him a beam of heav'nly fire;
Now in their mother's wombs, before their birth,
　Doth in all ſons of men their *Souls* inſpire.

And as *Minerva* is in fables ſaid,
　From *Jove*, without a mother, to proceed;
So our true *Jove*, without a mother's aid;
　Doth daily millions of *Minervas* breed.

SECT. V.

Erroneous Opinions of the Creation of
SOULS.

THEN neither from eternity before,
　Nor from the time, when *time's* firſt point begun,
Made he all *Souls*, which now he keeps in ſtore;
　Some in the moon, and others in the ſun:

Nor

Nor in a *secret cloyster* doth he keep
    Thefe virgin-fpirits, 'till their *marriage-day*;
Nor locks them up in chambers, where they fleep,
    Till they awake within thefe beds of clay,

Nor did he firft a certain number make,
    Infufing part in *beafts* and part in *men*;
And, as unwilling further pains to take,
    Would make no more than thofe he framed then.

So that the widow *Scul*, her Body dying,
    Unto the next born Body married was;
And fo by often changing, and fupplying,
    Men's *Souls* to beafts, and beafts to men did pafs.

(Thefe thoughts are fond; for fince the Bodies born
    Be more in number far, than thofe that die,
Thoufands muft be abortive, and forlorn
    Ere others deaths to them their *Souls* fupply:)

But as *God's handmaid, nature*, doth create
    Bodies in time diftinct, and order due;
So God gives *Souls* the like fucceffive date,
    Which *himfelf* makes, in Bodies formed new,

Which

Which *himself* makes of no material thing ;
 For unto angels he no pow'r hath giv'n
Either to fórm the fhape, or ftuff to bring
 From *air or fire, or fubftance of the heav'n.*

Nor herein doth he *nature*'s fervice ufe ;
 For tho' from Bodies, fhe can Bodies bring,
Yet could fhe never Souls from Souls *traduce,*
 As fire from fire, or light from light doth fpring.

S E C T. VI.

That the S o u l *is not* ex traduce.

Alas ! that fome who were great lights of old,
 And in their hands the lamp of God did bear !
Some rev'rend fathers did this error hold,
 Having their eyes dimm'd with religious fear.

OBJEC-

OBJECTION.

For when (fay they) by rule of faith we find,
   That ev'ry *Soul* unto her Body knit,
Brings from the mother's womb the *fin of kind*,
   The *root* of all the *ill* fhe doth commit.

How can we fay that God the *Soul* doth make,
   But we muft make him author of her fin?
Then from man's *Soul* fhe doth beginning take,
   Since in man's *Soul* corruption did begin.

For if God make her firft he makes her ill,
   (Which God forbid our thoughts fhould yield
      unto;)
Or makes the Body her fair form to fpill,
   Which, of itfelf, it had not pow'r to do.

Not *Adam's Body*, but his *Soul* did fin,
   And fo herfelf unto corruption brought;
But our poor *Soul* corrupted is within,
   Ere fhe had finn'd, either in act, or thought:

And

And yet we see in her such pow'rs divine,
    As we could gladly think, *from God she came:*
:Fain would we make him author of the wine,
    ,If for the dregs we could some other blame.

A N S W E R.

Thus these good men with holy zeal were blind,
    When on the other part the truth did shine;
Whereof we do clear demonstrations find,
    By light of *nature*, and by light *divine*.

None are so gross as to contend for this,
    That Souls from Bodies may traduced be;
Between whose natures no proportion is,
    When root and branch in nature still agree.

But many subtle wits have justify'd,
    That *Souls* from *Souls* spiritually may spring;
Which (if the nature of the *Soul* be try'd)
    Will e'en in nature prove as gross a thing,

S E C T. VII.

Reasons drawn from Nature.

For all things made, are either made of nought,
    Or made of stuff that ready made doth stand:
Of nought no creature ever formed ought,
    For that is proper to th' Almighty's hand.

If then the *Soul* another *Soul* do make,
    Because her pow'r is kept within a bound,
She must some former stuff, or *matter* take;
    But in the *Soul* there is no *matter* found.

Then if her heav'nly form do not agree
    With any *matter* which the world contains,
Then she of *nothing* must created be;
    And to *create*, to God alone pertains.

Again, if *Souls* do other *Souls* beget,
    'Tis by themselves, or by the Body's pow'r:
If by themselves, what doth their working let,
    But they might *Souls* engender ev'ry hour?

If

If by the Body, how can *wit* and *will*
  Join with the Body only in this act,
Since when they do their other works fulfil,
  They from the Body do themfelves *abftract.*

Again, if *Souls* of *Souls* begotten were,
  Into each other they fhould change and move:
And *change* and *motion ftill corruption* bear;
  How fhall we then the *Soul* immortal prove?

If, laftly, *Souls* do generation ufe,
  Then fhould they fpread incorruptible feed:
What then becomes of that which they do lofe,
  When th' act of generation do not fpeed?

And tho' the *Soul* could caft fpiritual feed,
  Yet *would* fhe not, becaufe fhe *never dies*;
For mortal things defire their like to breed,
  That fo they may their kind immortalize.

Therefore the angels, fons of God are nam'd,
  And marry not, nor are in marriage giv'n:
Their *fpirits* and ours are of one *fubftance* fram'd,
  And have one father, e'en the *Lord of heaven*;

                                      Who

Who would at firſt, that in each other thing,
  The *earth* and *water* living *Souls* ſhould breed,
But that *man's Soul*, whom he would make their king,
  Should from himſelf immediately proceed.

And when he took the *woman* from *man's* ſide,
  Doubtleſs himſelf inſpir'd her *Soul* alone :
For 'tis not ſaid, he did *man's Soul* divide,
  But took *fleſh of his fleſh, bone of his bone.*

Laſtly, God being made man for man's own ſake,
  And being like man in all, except in ſin,
His Body from the *virgin's* womb did take ;
  But all agree, *God form'd his Soul within.*

Then is the *Soul* from God ; ſo *Pagans* ſay,
  Which ſaw by *nature's* light her heav'nly kind ;
Naming her *kin to God, and God's bright ray,*
  A citizen of heav'n, to earth confin'd.

But now I feel, they pluck me by the ear,
  Whom my young *muſe* ſo boldly termed blind !
And crave more heav'nly light, that cloud to clear ;
  Which makes them think, God doth not make the
    mind.
                              S E C T.

S E C T. VIII.

Reasons from Divinity.

GOD doubtless, makes her, and doth make her good,
  And grafts her in the Body, there to spring;
Which, though it be corrupted flesh and blood,
  Can no way to the Soul corruption bring:

Yet is not God the author of her *ill*,
  Though author of her *being*, and *being there*:
And if we dare to judge our *Maker*'s will,
  He can condemn us, and himself can clear.

First, God from infinite eternity
  Decreed, what *hath been*, *is*, or *shall be* done;
And was resolv'd, that ev'ry man should be,
  And in his turn, his race of life should run:

And so did purpose all the *Souls* to make,
  That ever *have been* made, or *ever shall*;
And that their *being* they should only take
  In human Bodies, or not *be* at all.

Was

'Was it then fit that fuch a weak event
    (*Weakneſs itſelf*, the fin and fall of man)
.His counſel's execution ſhould prevent,
    Decreed and fix'd before the world began ?

Or that one *penal law* by *Adam* broke,
    Should make God break his own *eternal law*;
.The ſettled order of the world revoke,
    And change all forms of things which he foreſaw?

Could *Eve*'s weak hand, extended to the tree,
    In ſunder rent that *adamantine chain*,
Whoſe golden links, *effects and cauſes* be;
    And which to God's own chair doth fix'd remain?

O could we fee how cauſe from cauſe doth ſpring!
    How mutually they link'd and folded are!
And hear how oft one diſagreeing ſtring
    The harmony doth rather make than mar!

And view at once, how *death* by *ſin* is brought;
    And how from *death*, a better *life* doth riſe!
How this God's *juſtice*, and his *mercy* taught!
    We this decree would praiſe, as right and wiſe.

                      But

But we that meafure times by firft and laft,
  The fight of things *fucceffively* do take,
When God on all at once his view doth caft,
  And of all times doth but one *inftant* make.

All in *Himfelf*, as in a *glafs*, he fees;
  For *from Him, by Him, thro' Him, all things be:*
His fight is not difcourfive, by degrees;
  But feeing th' whole, each fingle part doth fee.

He looks on *Adam*, as a *root*, or *well*;
  And on his heirs, as *branches*, and as *ftreams:*
He fees *all* men, as *one* man, though they dwell
  In fundry cities, and in fundry realms.

And as the *root* and *branch* are but one *tree*,
  And *well* and *ftream* do but one *river* make;
So, if the *root* and *well* corrupted be,
  The *ftream* and *branch* the fame corruption take.

So, when the root and fountain of mankind
  Did draw corruption, and God's curfe, by fin;
This was a charge, that all his heirs did bind,
  And all his offspring grew corrupt therein.

And

And as when th' hand doth ſtrike, the man offends,
   (For part from whole, law ſevers not in this)
So *Adam*'s ſin to the whole kind extends ;
   For all their natures are but part of his.

Therefore this *ſin of kind*, not perſonal,
   But real, and hereditary was ;
The guilt thereof, and puniſhment to all,
   By courſe of nature, and of law doth paſs.

For as that eaſy law was giv'n to all,
   To anceſtor and heir, to firſt and laſt ;
So was the firſt tranſgreſſion general ;
   And all did pluck the fruit, and all did taſte.

Of this we find ſome foot-ſteps in our law,
   Which doth her root from God and nature take ;
Ten thouſand men ſhe doth together draw,
   And of them all, one corporation make ;

Yet theſe, and their ſucceſſors, are but one ;
   And if they gain, or loſe their liberties,
They harm, or profit not themſelves alone,
   But ſuch as in ſucceeding times ſhall riſe.

And

And fo the anceſtor, and all his heirs,
   Though they in number paſs the ſtars of heav'n,
Are ſtill but one ; his forfeitures are theirs,
   And unto them are his advancements giv'n :

His civil acts do bind and bar them all ;
   And as from *Adam*, all corruption take,
So, if the father's crime be *capital*,
   In all the *blood*, law doth corruption make.

Is it then juſt with us, to diſinherit
   Th' unborn nephews, for the father's fault ;
And to advance again, for one man's merit,
   A thouſand heirs that have deſerved nought ?

And is not God's decree as juſt as ours,
   If he, for *Adam*'s ſin, his ſons deprive
Of all thoſe native virtues, and thoſe pow'rs,
   Which he to him, and to his race did give ?

For, what is this contagious ſin of kind,
   But a *privation* of that grace within,
And of that great rich dowry of the mind,
   Which all had had, but for the firſt man's ſin.

If

If then a man, on light conditions gain'
   A great eftate, to him, and his, for ever;
If wilfully he forfeit it again,
   Who doth bemoan his heir or blame the giver;

So, though God make the *Soul* good, rich and fair,
   Yet when her form is to the Body knit,
Which makes the man, which man is *Adam's heir*,
   Juftly forthwith he takes his grace from it :

And then the *Soul*, being firft from nothing brought,
   When God's grace fails her, doth to nothing fall ;.
And this *declining pronenefs unto nought*,
   Is e'en that *fin* that we are born withal.

Yet not alone the firft good qualities,
   Which in the firft *Soul* were, deprived are ;
But in their place the contrary do rife,
   And real fpots of fin her beauty mar.

Nor is it ftrange, that *Adam's* ill defert
   Should be transferr'd unto his guilty race,
When *Chrift* his grace and juftice doth impart
   To men unjuft, and fuch as have no grace.

Laftly,

Lastly, the *Soul* were better so to be
    Born slave to sin, than not to be at all;
Since (if she do believe) one sets her free,
    That makes her mount the higher for her fall.

Yet this the curious wits will not content;
    They yet will know (since God foresaw this ill)
Why his high providence did not prevent
    The declination of the first man's will.

If by his word he had the current stay'd
    Of *Adam*'s will, which was by nature free,
It had been one, as if his word had said,
    I will henceforth, that *man no man shall be.*

For what is man without a moving mind,
    Which hath a judging *wit*, and chusing *will?*
Now, if God's pow'r should her election bind,
    Her motions then would cease and stand all still.

And why did God in man this *Soul* infuse,
    But that he should his Maker *know and love?*
Now, if *love* be compell'd, and cannot chuse,
    How can it grateful, or thank-worthy prove?

                            Love

Love muſt free-hearted be, and voluntary;
   And not inchanted, or by fate conſtrain'd :
Nor like that love, which did *Ulyſſes* carry
   To *Circe's* iſle, with mighty charms enchain'd.

Beſides, were we unchangeable in *will*,
   And of a *wit* that nothing could miſ-deem;
Equal to God ; whoſe wiſdom ſhineth ſtill,
   And never errs, we might ourſelves eſteem.

So that if man would be unvariable,
   He muſt be God, or like a rock or tree ;
For e'en the perfect angels were not ſtable,
   But had a fall more deſperate than we.

Then let us praiſe that pow'r, which makes us be
   Men as we are, and reſt contented ſo ;
And knowing man's fall was curioſity,
   Admire God's counſels, which we cannot know.

And let us know that God the maker is
   Of all the *Souls*, in all the men that be;
Yet their corruption is no fault of his,
   But the firſt man's that broke God's firſt decree.

S E C T. IX.

Why the Soul is united to the Body.

THIS *substance*, and this *spirit of God's own making*,
  Is in the Body plac'd, and planted here,
" That both of God, and of the world partaking,
" Of all that is, man might the image bear."

God first made angels bodiless, pure minds ;
  Then other things, which mindless Bodies be ;
Last, he made man, th' *horizon* 'twixt both kinds,
  In whom we do the world's abridgment see.

Besides, this world below did need *one wight*,
  Which might thereof distinguish ev'ry part ;
Make use thereof, and take therein delight ;
  And order things with industry and art :

Which also God might in his works admire,
  And here beneath yield him both pray'r and praise ;
As there, above, the holy angels choir
  Doth spread his glory forth with spiritual lays.

Lastly,

Laſtly, the brute, unreaſonable wights,
  Did want a *viſible king*, o'er them to reign :
And God himſelf thus to the world unites,
  That ſo the world might endleſs bliſs obtain.

SECT. X.

In what manner the SOUL *is united to the Body.*

B U T how ſhall we this *union* well expreſs ?
  Naught ties the *Soul*, her ſubtlety is ſuch ;
:She moves the Body, which ſhe doth poſſeſs ;
  Yet no part toucheth, but by *virtue*'s touch.

Then dwells ſhe not therein, as in a *tent* ;
  Nor as a pilot in his *ſhip* doth ſit ;
Nor as the ſpider in his *web* is pent ;
  Nor as the wax retains the print in it ;

E 2   Nor

Nor as a veſſel water doth contain ;
 Nor as one liquor in another ſhed ;
Nor as the heat doth in the fire remain ;
 Nor as a voice throughout the air is ſpread:

But as the fair and chearful *morning light*
 Doth here and there her ſilver-beams impart,
And in an inſtant doth herſelf unite
 To the tranſparent air, in all, and ev'ry part :

Still reſting whole, when blows the air divide ;
 Abiding pure, when th' air is moſt corrupted ;
Throughout the air, her beams diſperſing wide ;
 And when the air is toſs'd, not interrupted :

So doth the piercing *Soul* the Body fill,
 Being *all* in *all*, and all in part diffus'd ;
Indiviſible, incorruptible ſtill ;
 Not forc'd, encounter'd, troubled or confus'd.

And as the *ſun* above the light doth bring,
 Though we behold it in the air below ;
So from th' Eternal Light the *Soul* doth ſpring,
 Though in the Body ſhe her pow'rs do ſhow.

SECT.

S E C T. XI.

How the SOUL *exercises her Powers in the Body.*

*B*UT *as* the world's *fun* doth effect beget
 Diff 'rent, in divers places ev'ry day ;
Here *Autumn*'s temperature, there *Summer*'s heat ;
 Here flow'ry *Spring-tide*, and there *Winter* gray.

Here *ev'n,* there *morn* ; here *noon,* there *day,* there
  night,
 Melts wax, dries clay, makes flow'rs, fome quick,
  fome dead ;
Makes the *Moor* black, the *European* white ;
 Th' *American* tawny, and th' *Eaft-Indian* red :

So in our little world, this *Soul* of ours
 Being only one, and to one Body ty'd,
Doth ufe, on divers objects, divers powers ;
 And fo are her effects diverfify'd.

S E C T. XII.

The Vegetative Power of the SOUL.

*H*E R *quick'ning* power in ev'ry living part,
    Doth as a nurfe, or as a mother ferve ;
And doth employ her *œconomic art*,
    And bufy care, her houfhold to preferve.

Here fhe *attracts*, and there fhe doth *retain* ;
    There fhe *decocts*, and doth the food prepare ;
There fhe *diftributes* it to ev'ry vein,
    There fhe *expels* what fhe may fitly fpare.

This pow'r to *Martha* may compared be,
    Who bufy was, the *houfhold-things* to do :
Or to a *Dryas*, living in a tree :
    For e'en to trees this pow'r is proper too.

And though the *Soul* may not this pow'r extend
    Out of the Body, but ftill ufe it there ;
She hath a pow'r which fhe *abroad* doth fend,
    Which views and fearcheth all things ev'ry where.

SECT. XIII.

The Power of SENSE.

THIS pow'r is *Sense*, which from abroad doth bring
 The *colour*, *taste*, and *touch*, and *scent*, and *sound*,
The *quantity* and *shape* of ev'ry thing
 Within earth's centre, or heav'ns circle found.

This pow'r, in parts made fit, fit objects takes;
 Yet not the things, but forms of things receives;
As when a seal in wax impression makes,
 The print therein, but not itself, it leaves.

And though things *sensible* be numberless,
 But only five the *Sense's* organs be;
And in those five, all things their *forms* express,
 Which we can *touch*, *taste*, *feel*, or *hear*, or *see*.

These are the windows, thro' the which she views
 The *light of knowledge*, which is life's load-star:
" And yet while she these spectacles doth use,
 " Oft worldly things seem greater than they are."

S E C T. XIV.

SEEING.

*F*IRST, The two *Eyes*, which have the *seeing*
    pow'r,
    Stand as one watchman, spy or sentinel,
Being plac'd aloft, within the head's high tow'r;
    And tho' both see, yet both but one thing tell.

These mirrors take into their little space
    The forms of *moon* and *sun*, and ev'ry *star*,
Of ev'ry Body, and of ev'ry place,
    Which with the world's wide arms embraced are:

Yet their best object, and their noblest use,
    Hereafter in another world will be,
When God in them shall heav'nly light infuse,
    That face to face they may their *Maker* see.

Here are they guides, which do the Body lead,
    Which else would stumble in eternal night:
Here in this world they do much knowledge *read*,
    And are the casements which admit most light:

                They

They are her fartheſt reaching inſtrument,
 Yet they no beams unto their objects ſend;
But all the rays are from their objects ſent,
 And in the *Eyes* with pointed angles end.

If th' objects be far off, the rays do meet
 In a ſharp point, and ſo things ſeem but ſmall:
If they be near, their rays do ſpread and fleet,
 And make broad points, that things ſeem great
  withal.

Laſtly, nine things to *Sight* required are;
 The *pow'r* to ſee, the *light*, the *viſible* thing,
Being not too *ſmall*, too *thin*, too *nigh*, too *far*,
 Clear ſpace and *time*, the form diſtinct to bring.

Thus ſee we how the *Soul* doth uſe the eyes,
 As inſtruments of her quick pow'r of Sight;
Hence doth th' arts *optick*, and fair *painting* riſe;
 Painting, which doth all gentle minds delight.

S E C T.

SECT. XV.

HEARING.

NOW let us hear how she the *Ears* employs:
    Their office is, the troubled air to take;
Which in their mazes forms a found or noife,
    Whereof herfelf doth true diftinction make.

Thefe wickets of the *Soul* are plac'd on high,
    Becaufe all founds do lightly mount aloft;
And that they may not pierce too *violently*,
    They are *delay'd* with *turns* and *windings* oft.

For fhould the voice directly ftrike the brain,
    It would aftonifh and confufe it much;
Therefore thefe plaits and folds the found reftrain,
    That it the *organ* may more *gently* touch.

As ftreams, which with their winding banks do play,
    Stopp'd by their creeks, run foftly thro' the plain:
So in th' Ear's *labyrinth* the voice doth ftray,
    And doth with *eafy* motion touch the brain.

This

This is the floweft, yet the daintieft *fenfe*;
  For e'en the *Ears* of fuch as have no fkill,
Perceive a difcord, and conceive offence;
  And knowing not what's *good*, yet find the *ill*.

And tho' this *fenfe* firft gentle mufic found,
  Her proper object is *the fpeech of men*;
But that fpeech chiefly which God's heralds found,
  When their tongues utter what his fpirit did pen.

Our *Eyes* have lids, our *Ears* ftill ope we fee,
  Quickly to hear how ev'ry tale is prov'd:
Our *Eyes* ftill move, our *Ears* unmoved be;
  That tho' we hear quick, we be not quickly mov'd.

Thus by the organs of the *Eye* and *Ear*,
  The *Soul* with knowledge doth herfelf endue:
" Thus fhe her *prifon* may with pleafure bear,
  " Having fuch *profpects*, all the world to view."

Thefe *conduit-pipes* of knowledge feed the mind,
  But th' other three attend the Body ftill;
For by their fervices the *Soul* doth find,
  What things are to the Body good or ill.

SECT.

SECT. XVI.

TASTE.

*T*HE *Body*'s life with meats and air is fed,
  Therefore the *Soul* doth ufe the *tafting* pow'r.
In veins, which thro' the tongue and palate fpread,
  Diftinguifh ev'ry relifh, fweet and four.

This is the Body's *nurfe* ; but fince man's wit
  Found th' art of *cook'ry* to delight his *fenfe*,
More Bodies are confum'd and kill'd with it,
  Than with the fword, famine, or peftilence.

SECT. XVII.

SMELLING.

*N*EXT, in the noftrils fhe doth ufe the *Smell* :
  As God the *breath of life* in them did give ;
So makes he now this pow'r in them to dwell,
  To judge all airs, whereby we *breathe* and *live*.

This

This *sense* is also mistress of an art,
  Which to soft people sweet perfumes doth sell ;
Tho' this dear art doth little good impart,
  " Since they smell best, that do of nothing smell."

And yet good *scents* do purify the brain,
  Awake the *fancy*, and the wits refine :
Hence old *devotion*, *incense* did ordain,
  To make men's spirits apt for thoughts divine.

SECT. XVIII.

FEELING.

*L*ASTLY, *The feeling pow'r*, which is life's root,
  Thro' ev'ry living part itself doth shed
By *sinews*, which extend from head to foot ;
  And like a net, all o'er the Body spread.

Much like a ſubtle ſpider, * which doth ſit
   In middle of her web, which ſpreadeth wide ;
If aught do touch the utmoſt *thread* of it,
   She *feels* it inſtantly on ev'ry ſide.

By *touch*, the firſt pure qualities we learn,
   Which quicken all things, *hot, cold, moiſt* and *dry ;*
By *touch*, *hard, ſoft, rough, ſmooth*, we do diſcern :
   By *touch*, *ſweet pleaſure*, and *ſharp pain* we try.

---

* " The ſpider's touch how exquiſitely fine,
   " Feels at each thread, and lives along the line."

                    Pope's Eſſay on Man.

SECT.

S E C T. XIX.

Of the IMAGINATION, *or Common Senfe.*

THESE are the outward inftruments of *Senfe;*
 Thefe are the *guards* which ev'ry thing muft pafs,
Ere it approach the mind's intelligence,
 Or touch the fantafy, *wit's looking-glafs.*

And yet thefe porters, which all things admit,
 Themfelves perceive not, nor difcern the things :
One *common* pow'r doth in the *forehead* fit,
 Which all their proper *forms* together brings.

For all thofe *nerves,* which *fpirits of Senfe* do bear,
 And to thofe outward *organs* fpreading go,
United are, as in a *centre,* there ;
 And there this *pow'r* thofe fundry *forms* doth know.

Thofe outward organs prefent things receive,
 This inward *Senfe* doth abfent things retain ;
Yet ftrait tranfmits all forms fhe doth perceive,
 Unto an higher region of the *brain.*

S E C T.

SECT. XX.

FANTASY.

WHERE *Fantasy*, near *hand-maid* to the mind,
  Sits, and beholds, and doth discern them all;
Compounds in one, things diff'rent in their kind;
  Compares the black and white, the great and small.

Besides, those single forms she doth esteem,
  And in her balance doth their values try;
Where some things good, and some things ill do seem,
  And neutral some, in her *fantastick eye*.

This busy pow'r is working day and night;
  For when the outward *senses* rest do take,
A thousand dreams, fantastical and light,
  With flutt'ring wings, do keep her still awake.

SECT.

SECT, XXI.

SENSITIVE MEMORY.

YET always all may not afore her be ;
  Succeſſively ſhe this and that intends ;
Therefore ſuch forms as ſhe doth ceaſe to ſee,
  To *Memory's* large volume ſhe commends.

This *ledger-book* lies in the brain behind,
  Like *Janus'* eye, which in his poll was ſet :
The *layman's tables, ſtorehouſe of the mind ;*
  Which doth remember much, and much forget.

Here *ſenſe's apprehenſion* end doth take ;
  As when a ſtone is into water caſt,
One circle doth another circle make,
  Till the laſt circle touch the bank at laſt.

F   SECT.

SECT. XXII.

The *Passion* of the SENSE.

BUT tho' the *apprehensive pow'r* do pause,
  The *motive* virtue then begins to move ;
Which in the heart below doth *Passions* cause,
  Joy, grief, and *fear,* and *hope,* and *hate,* and *love.*

These Passions have a free commanding might,
  And divers actions in our life do breed ;
For all acts done without true *reason's* light,
  Do from the *passion* of the *Sense* proceed.

But since the *brain* doth lodge the pow'rs of *Sense,*
  How makes it in the *heart* those passions spring ?
The mutual love, the kind *intelligence*
  'Twixt *heart* and *brain,* this *sympathy* doth bring.

From the kind heat, which in the heart doth reign,
  The *spirits* of life do their beginning take ;
These *spirits* of life ascending to the brain,
  When they come there, the *spirits* of *Sense* do make.

These

Thefe *fpirits* of *Senfe*, in fantafy's high court,
    Judge of the forms of *objects*, ill or well ;
And fo they fend a good or ill report
    Down to the *heart*, where all *affections* dwell.

If the report be *good*, it caufeth *love*,
    And longing *hope*, and well affured *joy* ;
If it be *ill*, then doth it *hatred* move,
    And trembling *fear*, and vexing *griefs* annoy.

Yet were thefe natural affections good,
    (For they which want them, *blocks* or *devils* be)
If *reafon* in her firft perfection ftood,
    That fhe might *nature's* paffions rectify.

S E C T. XXIII.

LOCAL MOTION.

BESIDES, another *motive*-power doth arife
    Out of the heart, from whofe pure blood do fpring
The *vital fpirits* ; which born in *arteries*,
    Continual motion to all parts do bring.

This

This makes the pulfes beat, and lungs refpire :
   This holds the finews like a bridle's reins ;
And makes the Body to advance, retire,
   To turn, or ftop, as fhe them flacks, or ftrains.

Thus the *Soul* tunes the *Body*'s inftruments,
   Thefe harmonies fhe makes with *life* and *fenfe* ;
The organs fit are by the Body lent,
   But th' *aƐions* flow from the *Soul*'s influence.

S E C T.   XXIV.

The intelleƐual Powers of the S O U L.

B U T *now* I have a *will*, yet want a *wit*,
   T' exprefs the working of the *wit* and *will* ;
Which, though their *root* be to the body knit,
   Ufe not the body, when they ufe their *fkill.*

Thefe pow'rs the nature of the *Soul declare*,
   For to man's *Soul* thefe only proper be ;
For on the earth no other wights there are
   That have thefe heav'nly powers, but only we.

S E C T.

S E C T. XXV.

*Wit, Reafon, Underftanding, Opinion,
Judgment, Wifdom.*

THE *Wit,* the pupil of the *Soul's* clear eye,
   And in man's world, the only fhining *ftar,*
Looks in the *mirror* of the *fantafy,*
   Where all the *gath'rings* of the *fenfes* are.

From thence this *pow'r* the *fhapes* of things abftracts,
   And them within her *paffive part* receives,
Which are enlight'ned by that part which acts;
   And fo the *forms* of fingle things perceives.

But after, by difcourfing to and fro,
   Anticipating, and comparing things,
She doth all *univerfal* natures know,
   And all *effects* into their *caufes* bring.

When fhe *rates* things, and moves from ground to
      ground,
   The name of *Reafon* fhe obtains by this:
But when by *Reafon* fhe the truth hath found,
   And *ftandeth fix'd;* fhe *Underftanding* is.

When

When her aſſent ſhe *lightly* doth incline
    To either part, ſhe his *opinion's light :*
But when ſhe doth by principles define
    A certain *truth,* ſhe hath *true Judgment's* ſight.

And as from *ſenſes,* *Reaſon's* work doth ſpring,
    So many *Reaſons Underſtanding* gain ;
And many *Underſtandings, knowledge* bring,
    And by much *knowledge, Wiſdom* we obtain.

So, many ſtairs we muſt aſcend upright,
    Ere we attain to *Wiſdom's* high degree :
So doth this earth eclipſe our Reaſon's light,
    Which elſe (in inſtants) would like angels ſee.

SECT. XXVI.

Innate Ideas in the SOUL.

YET hath the *Soul* a dowry natural,
    And *ſparks of light,* ſome common things to ſee ;
Not being a blank where naught is writ at all,
    But what the writer will, may written be.

                            For

For nature in man's heart her laws doth pen,
  Prefcribing *truth* to *wit*, and *good* to *will*;
Which do *accufe*, or elfe *excufe* all men,
  For ev'ry thought or practice, good or ill:

And yet thefe fparks grow almoft infinite,
  Making the world, and all therein, their food;
As fire fo fpreads, as no place holdeth it,
  Being nourifh'd ftill with new *fupplies* of wood.

And tho' thefe fparks were almoft quench'd with *fin*,
  Yet they whom that *juft One* hath juftify'd,
Have them increas'd with heav'nly light within;
  And like the *widow's oil*, ftill *multiply'd*.

S E C T. XXVII.

The Power of WILL, *and Relation between*
the WIT *and* WILL.

A N D as this *Wit* fhould *goodnefs* truly know,
  We have a *Will*, which that true good fhould chufe,
Tho' *Will* do oft (when *Wit* falfe forms doth fhow)
  Take *ill* for *good*, and *good* for *ill* refufe.

Will puts in practice what the *Wit* deviseth :
　　Will ever acts, and *Wit* contemplates still :
And as from *Wit*, the pow'r of *wisdom* riseth,
　　All other virtues daughters are of *Will*.

Will is the *prince*, and *Wit* the *counsellor*,
　　Which doth for *common good* in council sit ;
And when *Wit* is resolv'd, *Will* lends her pow'r
　　To execute what is advis'd by *Wit*.

Wit is the mind's chief judge, which doth controul
　　Of *fancy*'s court the judgments false and vain :
Will holds the royal scepter in the *Soul*,
　　And on the *passions* of the heart doth reign.

Will is as free as any *emperor*,
　　Naught can restrain her *gentle* liberty :
No tyrant, nor no torment hath the pow'r
　　To make us *will*, when we unwilling be.

SECT.

S E C T. XXVIII.

The Intellectual Memory.

To thefe high pow'rs a *ſtore-houſe* doth pertain,
    Where they all arts, and *gen'ral* reaſons lay;
Which in the *Soul*, e'en after *death*, remain,
    And no *Lethean* flood can waſh away.

S E C T. XXIX.

The Dependency of the S o u l's Faculties
upon each other.

This is the *Soul*, and theſe her *virtues* be;
    Which, though they have their ſundry proper ends,
And one exceeds another in *degree*,
    Yet each *on other* mutually depends.

Our wit is giv'n *Almighty God* to *know*;
    Our *will* is giv'n to *love* him, being *known*:
But God could not be *known* to us below,
    But by his *works*, which thro' the ſenſe are ſhown.

And

And as the *wit* doth reap the fruits of *sense*,
   So doth the *quick'ning* pow'r the *senses feed:*
Thus while they do their sundry gifts dispense,
   " The best the service of the least doth need."

Ev'n so the king his magistrates do serve,
   Yet commons feed both magistrates and king:
The common's peace the magistrates preserve,
   By borrow'd pow'r, which from the prince doth
      spring.

The *quick'ning power* would *be*, and so would rest;
   The *sense* would not *be* only, but *be well:*
But *wit's* ambition longeth to the best,
   For it desires in *endless* bliss to dwell.

And these three pow'rs three sorts of men do make;
   For some, like plants, their veins do only fill;
And some, like beasts, their senses pleasure take;
   And some, like angels, do contemplate still.

Therefore the fables turn'd some men to flow'rs,
   And others did with brutish forms invest;
And did of others make celestial pow'rs,
   Like angels, which still travel, yet still rest.

                           Yet

Yet thefe three pow'rs are not three *Souls*, but one ;
 As one and two are both contain'd in *three* ;
Three being one number by itfelf alone,
 A fhadow of the bleffed Trinity.

Oh ! *what* is man (great Maker of mankind !)
 That thou to him fo great refpect doft bear !
That thou adorn'ft him with fo bright a mind,
 Mak'ft him a king, and e'en an angel's peer !

Oh ! what a lively life, what heav'nly pow'r,
 What fpreading virtue, what a fparkling fire,
How great, how plentiful, how rich a dow'r
 Doft thou within this dying flefh infpire !

Thou leav'ft thy print in other works of thine ;
 But thy whole image thou in man haft writ :
There cannot be a creature more divine,
 Except (like thee) it fhould be infinite.

But it exceeds man's thought, to think how high
 God hath rais'd *man*, fince *God* a *man* became :
The angels do admire this *Myftery*,
 And are aftonifh'd when they view the fame.

Nor

Nor hath he giv'n thefe bleffings for a day,
   Nor made them on the Body's life depend :
The *Soul*, tho' made in time, *furvives for ay* ;
   And tho' it hath beginning, fees no end.

S E C T. XXX.

That the S O U L *is immortal, proved by*
feveral Reafons.

HE R only *end*, is *never-ending* bliſs ;
   Which is, *the eternal face of God to fee* ;
Who, *laſt of ends*, and *firſt of caufes is :*
   And to do this, ſhe muſt *eternal* be.

How fenfelefs then, and dead a *Soul* hath he,
   Which *thinks* his *Soul* doth with his Body die :
Or *thinks* not fo, but fo would have it be,
   That he might fin with more fecurity ?

For tho' thefe light and vicious perfons fay,
   Our *Soul* is but a fmoak, or airy blaſt,
Which, during life, doth in our noſtrils play ;
   And when we die, doth turn to wind at laſt :

                          Although

Although they fay, *come let us eat and drink* ;
　Our life is but a fpark, which quickly dies:
Though thus they *fay*, they know not what to *think* ;
　But in their minds ten thoufand doubts arife.

Therefore no hereticks defire to fpread
　Their light opinions, like thefe *epicures* ;
For fo their ftagg'ring thoughts are comforted,
　And other men's affent their doubt affures.

Yet tho' thefe men againft their confcience ftrive,
　There are fome fparkles in their flinty breafts,
Which cannot be extinct, but ftill revive ;
　That tho' they would, they cannot quite be *beafts.*

But whofo makes a mirror of his mind,
　And doth with patience view himfelf therein,
His *Soul's* eternity fhall clearly find,
　Tho' th' other beauties be defac'd with fin.

REASON

REASON I.

Drawn from the desire of Knowledge.

First, in man's mind we find an appetite
  To *learn* and *know the Truth* of ev'ry thing,
Which is co-natural, and born with it,
  And from the *essence* of the *Soul* doth spring.

With this *desire,* she hath a native *might*
  To find out ev'ry truth, if she had time;
Th' innumerable effects to sort aright,
  And by degrees, from cause to cause to climb.

But since our life so fast away doth slide,
  As doth a hungry eagle thro' the wind;
Or as a ship transported with the tide,
  Which in their passage leave no print behind;

Of which swift little time so much we spend,
  While some few things we thro' the sense do strain,
That our short race of life is at an end,
  Ere we the principles of skill attain.

Or God

Or God (who to vain ends hath nothing done)
   In vain this *appetite* and *pow'r* hath giv'n ;
Or elfe our knowledge, which is here begun,
   Hereafter muft be perfected in heav'n.

God never gave a *pow'r* to one whole kind,
   But moft part of that kind did ufe the fame :
Moft eyes have perfect fight, though fome be blind ;
   Moft legs can nimbly run, tho' fome be lame.

But in this life no *Soul* the truth can know
   So perfectly, as it hath pow'r to do :
If then perfection be not found below,
   An higher place muft make her mount thereto.

Reason II.

Drawn from the Motion of the Soul.

Again, how can fhe but immortal be,
   When with the motions of both *will* and *wit*,
She ftill afpireth to eternity,
   And never refts, till fhe attain to it ?

Water in conduit-pipes, can rife no higher
  Than the well-head, from whence it firft doth fpring :
Then fince to eternal *God* fhe doth afpire,
  She cannot be but an eternal thing.

" All moving things to other things do move,
  " Of the fame kind which fhews their nature fuch :"
So *earth* falls down, and *fire* doth mount above,
  Till both their proper elements do touch.

And as the moifture, which the thirfty earth
  Sucks from the fea, to fill her empty veins,*
From out her womb at laft doth take a birth,
  And runs a *lymph* along the graffy plains :

Long doth fhe ftay, as loth to leave the land,
  From whofe foft fide fhe firft did iffue make :
She taftes all places, turns to ev'ry hand,
  Her flow'ry banks unwilling to forfake :

---

* The Soul compared to a river.

Yet

Yet *nature* fo her ftreams doth lead and carry,
  As that her courfe doth make no final ftay,
Till fhe herfelf unto the *ocean* marry,
  Within whofe watry bofom firft fhe lay.

E'en fo the *Soul*, which in this earthly mould
  The Spirit of God doth fecretly infufe,
Becaufe at firft fhe doth the earth behold,
  And only this material world fhe views :

At firft her *mother-earth* fhe holdeth dear,
  And doth embrace the world, and worldly things ;
She flies clofe by the ground, and hovers here,
  And mounts not up with her celeftial wings :

Yet under heav'n fhe cannot light on aught
  That with her heav'nly *nature* doth agree ;
She cannot reft, fhe cannot fix her thought,
  She cannot in this world contented be.

For who did ever yet, in *honour*, *wealth*,
  Or *pleafure of the fenfe*, contentment find ?
Who ever ceas'd to wifh, when he had *health* ?
  Or having *wifdom*, was not vex'd in mind ?

G   Then

Then as a *bee* which among weeds doth fall,
　　Which feem fweet flow'rs, with luftre frefh and gay;
She lights on that, and this, and tafteth all;
　　But pleas'd with none, doth rife, and foar away:

So, when the *Soul* finds here no true content,
　　And, like *Noah*'s dove, can no fure footing take,
She doth return from whence fhe firft was fent,
　　And flies to *him* that firft her wings did make.

Wit, feeking *truth*, from caufe to caufe afcends,
　　And never refts, till it the *firft* attain:
Will, feeking *good*, finds many middle ends;
　　But never ftays, till it the *laft* do gain.

Now *God* the *Truth*, and *Firft of Caufes is*;
　　God is the *laft good end*, which lafteth ftill;
Being *Alpha* and *Omega* nam'd for this;
　　Alpha to *Wit*, *Omega* to the *Will*.

Since then her heav'nly kind fhe doth difplay,
　　In that to *God* fhe doth directly move;
And on no mortal thing can make her ftay,
　　She cannot be from hence, but from *above*.

　　　　　　　　　　　　　　　　And

And yet this *first true cause*, and *last good end*,
  She cannot here so *well*, and *truly* see;
For this perfection she must yet attend,
  Till to her *Maker* she espoused be.

As a *king*'s daughter, being in person sought
  Of divers princes, who do neighbour near,
On none of them can fix a constant thought,
  Though she to all do lend a gentle ear:

Yet she can love a foreign *emperor*,
  Whom of great worth and pow'r she hears to be,
If she be woo'd but by *ambassador*,
  Or but his *letters*, or his *pictures* see:

For well she knows, that when she shall be brought
  Into the *kingdom* where her *spouse* doth reign;
Her eyes shall see what she conceiv'd in thought,
  Himself, his state, his glory, and his train.

So while the *virgin-soul* on *earth* doth stay,
  She woo'd and tempted is ten thousand ways,
By these great pow'rs, which on the *earth* bear sway;
  The *wisdom of the world*, *wealth*, *pleasure*, *praise*:

With thefe fometimes fhe doth her time beguile,
    Thefe do by fits her fantafy poffefs;
But fhe diftaftes them all within awhile,
    And in the fweeteft finds a tedioufnefs.

But if upon the world's Almighty King
    She once doth fix her humble loving thought,
Who by his *picture* drawn in ev'ry thing,
    And *facred meffages*, her *love* hath fought;

Of him fhe thinks fhe cannot think too much;
    This honey tafted ftill, is ever fweet;
The pleafure of her ravifh'd thought is fuch,
    As almoft here fhe with her blifs doth meet:

But when in heav'n fhe fhall his *effence* fee,
    This is her *fov'reign good*, and *perfect blifs*;
Her longing, wifhings, hopes, all finifh'd be;
    Her joys are full, her motions reft in this:

There is fhe crown'd with garlands of *content*;
    There doth fhe manna eat, and nectar drink:
That prefence doth fuch high delights prefent,
    As never tongue could fpeak, nor heart could think.

REASON

REASON III.

*From Contempt of Death in the better Sort
of Spirits.*

For this, the better *Souls* do oft defpife
   The Body's death, and do it oft defire ;
For when on ground, the burthen'd balance lies,
   The empty part is lifted up the higher :

But if the Body's death the *Soul* fhould kill,
   Then death muft needs *againft her nature* be ;
And were it fo, all *Souls* would fly it ftill,
   For nature hates and fhuns her contrary.

For all things elfe, which nature makes to be,
   Their *being* to preferve, are chiefly taught ;
And tho' fome things defire a change to fee,
   Yet never thing did long to turn to naught.

If then by death the *Soul* were quenched quite,
   She could not thus againft her nature run ;
Since ev'ry fenfelefs thing, by nature's light,
   Doth prefervation feek, deftruction fhun.

Nor

Nor could the world's beft fpirits fo much err,
   If death took all, that they fhould all agree,
Before this life, their *honour* to prefer :
   For what is praife to things that nothing be ?

Again, if by the Body's prop fhe ftand ;
   If on the Body's life, her life depend,
As *Meleager*'s on the fatal brand,
   The Body's good fhe only would intend :

We fhould not find her half fo brave and bold,
   To lead it to the wars, and to the feas,
To make it fuffer watchings, hunger, cold,
   When it might feed with plenty, reft with eafe.

Doubtlefs, all *Souls* have a furviving thought,
   Therefore of death we think with quiet mind ;
But if we think of *being turn'd to naught*,
   A trembling horror in our *Souls* we find.

REASON

REASON IV.

From the Fear of Death in the wicked Souls.

And as the better spirit, when she doth bear
   A scorn of death, doth shew she cannot die;
So when the wicked *Soul* death's face doth fear,
   E'en then she proves her own eternity.

For when death's form appears, she feareth not
   An utter quenching or extinguishment;
She would be glad to meet with such a lot,
   That so she might all future ill prevent:

But she doth doubt what after may befall;
   For nature's law accuseth her within,
And faith, 'tis true what is affirm'd by all,
   That after death there is a pain for sin.

Then she who hath been hoodwink'd from her birth,
   Doth first herself within death's mirror see;
And when her Body doth return to earth,
   She first takes care, how she alone shall be.

Who ever fees thefe irreligious men,
 With burthen of a ficknefs weak and faint,
But hears them talking of religion then,
 And vowing of their *Souls* to ev'ry faint ?

When was there ever curfed *atheift* brought
 Unto the *gibbet*, but he did adore
That bleffed pow'r, which he had fet at naught,
 Scorn'd and blafphemed all his life before ?

Thefe light vain perfons ftill are drunk and mad,
 With furfeitings and pleafures of their youth ;
But at their death they are frefh, fober, fad ;
 Then they difcern, and then they fpeak the truth.

If then all *Souls*, both good and bad, do teach,
 With gen'ral voice, that *Souls* can never die ;
'Tis not man's flatt'ring glofs, but *nature's fpeech*,
 Which, like *God's* oracles, can never lie.

REASON V.

From the general Defire of Immortality.

Hence *fprings* that univerfal ftrong defire,
   Which all men have of immortality :
Not fome few fpirits unto this thought afpire,
   But all men's minds in this united be.

Then this defire of nature is not vain,
   " She covets not impoffibilities ;
" Fond thoughts may fall into fome idle brain,
   " But one *affent* of all, is ever wife."

From hence that gen'ral care and ftudy fprings,
   That *launching*, and *progreffion of the mind*,
Which all men have fo much of future things,
   That they no joy do in the prefent find.

From this defire, that main defire proceeds,
   Which all men have furviving fame to gain,
By *tombs*, by *books*, by memorable *deeds* ;
   For fhe that this defires, doth ftill remain.

Hence,

Hence, laftly, fprings care of pofterities,
    For things their kind would everlafting make::
Hence is it, that old men do plant young trees,,
    The fruit whereof another age fhall take.

If we thefe rules unto ourfelves apply,
    And view them by reflection of the mind,.
All thefe true notes of immortality
    In our *heart's tables* we fhall written find..

REASON VI..

From the very Doubt and Difputation of
Immortality.

And tho' fome impious wits do queftions move,
    And doubt if *Souls* immortal be, or no;
That *doubt* their immortality doth prove,
    Becaufe they feem immortal things to know..

For he who reafons on both parts doth bring,
    Doth fome things mortal, fome immortal call;.
Now, if himfelf were but a mortal thing,
    He could not judge immortal things at all.

                                      For

For when we judge, our minds we mirrors make;
   And as thofe glaffes which material be,
Forms of material things do only take;
   For *thoughts* or *minds* in them we cannot fee;

So when we God and angels do conceive,
   And think of *truth*, which is eternal too;
Then do our minds immortal forms receive,
   Which if they mortal were, they could not do.

And as if beafts conceiv'd what reafon were,
   And that conception fhould diftinctly fhow,
They fhould the name of *reafonable* bear;
   For without *reafon*, none could *reafon* know:

So when the *Soul* mounts with fo high a wing,
   As of eternal things fhe doubts can move;
She proofs of her eternity doth bring,
   Ev'n when fhe ftrives the contrary to prove.

For ev'n the *thought* of immortality,
   Being an act done without the Body's aid,
Shews, that herfelf alone could move and be,
   Although the Body in the grave were laid.

SECT.

S E C T. XXXI.

That the SOUL *cannot be deftroyed.*

AND if herfelf fhe can fo lively move,
  And never need a foreign help to take;
Then muft her motion everlafting prove,
  " Becaufe herfelf fhe never can forfake."

But tho' corruption cannot touch the mind,
  By any caufe * that from itfelf may fpring,
Some outward caufe fate hath perhaps defign'd,
  Which to the *Soul* may utter quenching bring.

Perhaps her caufe may ceafe, † and fhe may die;
  God is her *caufe,* his *word* her maker was;
Which fhall ftand fix'd for all eternity,
  When heav'n and earth fhall like a fhadow pafs.

---

  * Her caufe ceafeth not.   † She hath no contrary.

Perhaps

Perhaps fome thing repugnant to her kind,
   By ftrong *antipathy*, the *Soul* may kill :
But what can be *contrary* to the mind,
   Which holds all *contraries* in concord ftill ?

She lodgeth heat, and cold, and moift, and dry,
   And life and death, and peace, and war together;
Ten thoufand fighting things in her do lie,
   Yet neither troubleth, or difturbeth either.

Perhaps for want of food, the *Soul* may pine ;*
   But that were ftrange, fince all things *bad* and *good*;
Since all God's creatures, *mortal* and *divine* ;
   Since *God himfelf* is her eternal food.

Bodies are fed with things of mortal kind,
   And fo are fubject to mortality :
But *truth*, which is eternal, feeds the mind ;
   The *tree of life*, which will not let her die.

---

* She cannot die for want of food.

Yet violence, perhaps the *Soul* deftroys,* '
   As lightning, or the *fun-beams* dim the fight ;
Or as a thunder clap, or cannon's noife,
   The pow'r of hearing doth aftonifh quite :

But high perfection to the *Soul* it brings,
   T' encounter things moft excellent and high ;
For, when fhe views the beft and greateft things
   They do not hurt, but rather clear the eye.

Befides, as *Homer's gods,* 'gainft armies ftand,
   Her fubtle form can thro' all dangers flide :
Bodies are captive, minds endure no band ;
   " And will is free, and can no force abide."

But laftly, time perhaps at laft hath pow'r §
   To fpend her lively pow'rs, and quench her light ;
But old god *Saturn,* which doth all devour,
   Doth cherifh her, and ftill augment her might.

---

* Violence cannot deftroy her.
§ Time cannot deftroy her.

Heav'n

'Heav'n waxéth old, and all the *spheres* above
　Shall one day faint, and their fwift motion ftay ;
'And *time* itfelf, in time fhall ceafe to move ;
　Only the Soul furvives, and lives for ay.

" Our Bodies, ev'ry footftep that they make,
　" March towards death, until at laft they die :
" Whether we work or play, or fleep or wake,
　" Our life doth pafs, and with *time*'s wings doth
　　" fly :"

'But to the *Soul*, time doth perfection give,
　And adds frefh luftre to her beauty ftill ;
And makes her in eternal youth to live,
　Like her which nectar to the gods doth fill.

The more fhe lives, the more fhe feeds on *truth* ;
　The more fhe feeds, her *ftrength* doth more in-
　　creafe :
And what is *ftrength*, but an effect of *youth*,
　Which if *time* nurfe, how can it ever ceafe ?

SECT. XXXII.

Objections against the IMMORTALITY *of the*
SOUL, *with their respective answers.*

*B*UT *now* these *Epicures* begin to smile,
    And say, my doctrine is more safe than true ;
And that I fondly do myself beguile,
    While these receiv'd opinions I ensue.

OBJECTION I.

For, what, say they? doth not the *Soul* wax old?
    How comes it then that aged men do dote;
And that their brains grow sottish, dull and cold,
    Which were in youth the only spirits of note?

What? are not *Souls* within themselves corrupted?
    How can there ideots then by nature be?
How is it that some wits are interrupted,
    That now they dazzled are, now clearly see?

                              ANSWER.

ANSWER.

These questions make a subtil argument
  To such as think both *sense* and *reason* one ;
To whom nor agent, from the instrument,
  Nor pow'r of working, from the work is known.

But they that know that wit can shew no skill,
  But when she things in *sense's glass* doth view,
Do know, if accident this glass do spill,
  It *nothing sees,* or *sees the false for true.*

For, if that region of the tender brain,
  Where th' inward sense of fantasy should sit,
And th' outward senses, gath'rings should retain;
  By nature, or by chance, become unfit :

Either at first uncapable it is,
  And so few things, or none at all receives ;
Or mar'd by accident, which haps amiss ¡
  And so amiss it ev'ry thing perceives.

Then, as a cunning prince that useth *spies,*
  If they return no news, doth nothing know ;
But if they make advertisement of lies,
  The prince's counsels all awry do go:

·H   Ev'n

Ev'n fo the *Soul* to fuch a body knit,
 Whofe inward fenfes undifpofed be;
And to receive the forms of things unfit,
 Where nothing is brought in, can nothing fee.

This makes the idiot, which hath yet a mind,
 Able to *know* the truth, and *chufe* the good;
If fhe fuch figures in the brain did find,
 As might be found, if it in temper ftood.

But if a *phrenfy* do poffefs the brain,
 It fo difturbs and blots the forms of things,
As fantafy proves altogether vain,
 And to the wit no true relation brings.

Then doth the wit, admitting all for true,
 Build fond conclufions on thofe idle grounds:
Then doth it fly the good, and ill purfue;
 Believing all that this falfe *fpy* propounds.

But purge the humours, and the rage appeafe,
 Which this diftemper in the fanfy wrought;
Then fhall the *wit*, which never had difeafe,
 Difcourfe, and judge difcreetly, as it ought.

          So,

So, though the clouds eclipfe the *fun's* fair light,
 Yet from his face they do not take one beam;
So have our eyes their perfect pow'r of fight,
 Ev'n when they look into a troubled ftream.

Then thefe defects in *fenfe's* organs be,
 Not in the *Soul,* or in her working might:
She cannot lofe her perfect pow'r to fee,
 Though mifts and clouds do choak her window
  light.

Thefe imperfections then we muft impute,
 Not to the agent, but the inftrument:
We muft not blame *Apollo,* but his lute,
 If falfe accords from her falfe ftrings be fent.

The *Soul* in all hath one intelligence;
 Tho' too much moifture in an infant's brain,
And too much drynefs in an old man's fenfe,
 Cannot the prints of outward things retain:

Then doth the *Soul* want work, and idle fit,
 And this we *childifhnefs* and *dotage* call;
Yet hath fhe then a quick and active wit,
 If fhe had ftuff and tools to work withal:

For,

For, give her organs fit, and objects fair;
     Give but the aged man, the young man's fenfe;
Let but *Medea*, *Æfon*'s youth repair,
     And ftraight fhe fhews her wonted excellence.

As a good harper ftricken far in years,
     Into whofe cunning hands the gout doth fall,
All his old crotchets in his brain he bears,
     But on his harp plays ill, or not at all.

But if *Apollo* takes his gout away,
     That he his nimble fingers may apply;
Apollo's felf will envy at his play,
     And all the world applaud his minftrelfy.

Then *dotage* is no weaknefs of the mind,
     But of the *Senfe*; for if the mind did wafte,
In all old men we fhould this wafting find,
     When they fome certain term of years had pafs'd;

But moft of them, e'en to their dying hour,
     Retain a mind more lively, quick and ftrong;
And better ufe their underftanding pow'r,
     Then when their brains were warm, and limbs were
       young.

                                 For,

For, tho' the Body wafted be and weak,
    And tho' the leaden form of earth it bears ;
Yet when we hear that half dead Body fpeak,
    We oft are ravifh'd to the heav'nly *fpheres.*

OBJECTION II.

Yet fay thefe men, if all her organs die,
    Then hath the *Soul* no pow'r her pow'rs to ufe :
So, in a fort, her pow'rs extinct do lie,
    When unto *act* fhe cannot them reduce.

And if her pow'rs be dead, then what is fhe ?
    For fince from ev'ry thing fome *pow'rs* do fpring ;
And from thofe pow'rs, fome *acts* proceeding be ;
    Then kill both *pow'r* and *act*, and kill the thing.

ANSWER.

Doubtlefs, the Body's death, when once it dies,
    The inftruments of fenfe and life doth kill ;
So that fhe cannot ufe thofe faculties,
    Altho' their root reft in her fubftance ftill.

H 3

But

But (as the Body living) *wit* and *will*
   Can *judge* and *chufe*, without the Body's aid ;
Though on fuch objects they are working ftill,
   As thro' the Body's organs are convey'd :

So, when the Body ferves her turn no more,
   And all her *fenfes* are extinct and gone,
She can difcourfe of what fhe learn'd before,
   In heav'nly contemplations, all alone.

So, if one man well on the lute doth play,
   And have good horfemanfhip, and learning's fkill,
Though both his lute and horfe we take away,
   Doth he not keep his former learning ftill ?

He keeps it doubtlefs, and can ufe it too ;
   And doth both t'other *fkills* in pow'r retain ;
And can of both the proper actions do,
   If with his lute or horfe he meet again.

So tho' the inftruments, (by which we live,
   And view the world) the Body's death do kill ;
Yet with the Body they fhall all revive,
   And all their wonted offices fulfil.

O'BJEC-

OBJECTION III.

But how, till then, ſhall ſhe herſelf employ ?
  Her ſpies are dead, which brought home news be-
    fore :
What ſhe hath got, and keeps, ſhe may enjoy,
  But ſhe hath means to underſtand no more.

Then what do thoſe poor *Souls*, which nothing get ?
  Or what do thoſe which get, and cannot keep ?
Like bucklers bottomleſs, which all out-let ;
  Thoſe *Souls*, for want of exerciſe, muſt ſleep.

ANSWER.

See how man's *Soul* againſt itſelf doth ſtrive :
  Why ſhould we not have other means to know ?
As children, while within the womb they live,
  Feed by the navel : here they feed not ſo.

Theſe children, if they had ſome uſe of *ſenſe*,
  And ſhould by chance their mother's talking hear,
That in ſhort time they ſhall come forth from thence,
  Would fear their birth, more than our death we
    fear.

They

They would cry out, if we this place shall leave,
   Then shall we break our tender navel strings :
How shall we then our nourishment receive,
   Since our sweet food no other conduit brings ?

And if a man should to these babes reply,
   That into this fair world they shall be brought,
Where they shall view the earth, the sea, the sky,
   The glorious sun, and all that God hath wrought :

That there ten thousand dainties they shall meet,
   Which by their mouths they shall with pleasure take;
Which shall be cordial too, as well as sweet ;
   And of their little limbs, tall Bodies make :

This world they'd think a fable, e'en as we
   Do think the *story* of the *golden age* ;
Or as some sensual spirits 'mongst us be,
   Which hold the *world to come, a feigned stage* :

Yet shall these infants after find all true,
   Tho' then thereof they nothing could conceive :
As soon as they are born, the world they view,
   And with their mouths, the nurses milk receive.

So when the *Soul* is born (for death is naught
  But the *Soul's* birth, and so we should it call)
Ten thousand things she sees beyond her thought;
  And in an unknown manner, knows them all.

Then doth she see by spectacles no more,,
  She hears not by report of double spies;
Herself in instants doth all things explore;
  For each thing's present, and before her lies.

OBJECTION IV.

But still this crew with questions me pursues:
  If *Souls* deceas'd (say they) still living be,
Why do they not return, to bring us news
  Of that strange world, where they such wonders see?

ANSWER.

Fond men ! if we believe that men do live
  Under the *zenith* of both frozen *poles*,
Tho' none come thence, advertisement to give,
  Why bear we not the like faith of our *Souls ?*

                         The

The *Soul* hath here on earth no more to do,

    Than we have bufinefs in our mother's womb :

What child doth covet to return thereto,

    Although all children firft from thence do come?

But as *Noah*'s pigeon, which return'd no more,

    Did fhew, fhe footing found, for all the flood ;

So when good *Souls*, departed thro' death's door,

    Come not again it fhews their dwelling good.

And doubtlefs, fuch a *Soul* as up doth mount,

    And doth appear before her Maker's face,

Holds this vile world in fuch a bafe account,

    As fhe looks down and fcorns this wretched place.

But fuch as are detruded down to hell,

    Either for fhame, they ftill themfelves retire ;

Or ty'd in chains, they in clofe prifon dwell,

    And cannot come, although they much defire.

OBJEC-

OBJECTION V.

Well, well, fay thefe vain fpirits, though vain it is
  To think our *Souls* to heav'n or hell do go;
Politick men have thought it not amifs,
  To fpread this *lie,* to make men virtuous.fo.

ANSWER.

Do you then think this *moral virtue* good?
  I think you do, ev'n for your private gain;
For commonwealths by *virtue* ever ftood,
  And common good the private doth contain.

If then this *virtue* you do love fo well,
  Have you no means, her practice to maintain;
But you this *lie* muft to the people tell,
  That good *Souls* live in joy, and ill in pain?

Muft *virtue* be preferved by a *lie?*
  Virtue and *truth* do ever beft agree;
By this it feems to be a verity,
  Since the effects fo good and virtuous be.

For,

For, as the devil the father is of lies,
   So vice and mifchief do his lies enfue:
Then this good doctrine did not he devife;
   But made this *lie*, which faith, it is not true.

For, how can that be falfe, which ev'ry tongue
   Of ev'ry mortal man affirms for true?
Which truth hath in all ages been fo ftrong,
   As, load-ftone like, all hearts it ever drew.

For, not the *Chriftian*, or the *Jew* alone,
   The *Perfian*, or the *Turk*, acknowledge this;
This myftery to the wild *Indian* known,
   And to the *Canibal* and *Tartar* is.

This rich *Affyrian* drug grows ev'ry where;
   As common in the *North*, as in the *Eaft*:
This doctrine doth not enter by the *ear*,
   But of itfelf is native in the breaft.

None that acknowledge God, or providence,
   Their *Soul's* eternity did ever doubt;
For all *religion* taketh root from hence,
   Which no poor naked nation lives without.

For fince the world for man created was,
  (For only man the ufe thereof doth know)
If man do perifh like a wither'd grafs,
  How doth God's wifdom order things below ?

And if that wifdom ftill wife ends propound,
  Why made he man, of other creatures, king;
When (if he perifh here) there is not found
  In all the world fo poor and vile a thing?

If death do quench us quite, we have great wrong,
  Since for our fervice all things elfe were wrought;
That *daws*, and *trees*, and *rocks* fhould laft fo long,
  When we muft in an inftant pafs to naught.

But blefs'd be that *Great Pow'r*, that hath us blefs'd
  With longer life than heav'n or earth can have;
Which hath infus'd into our mortal breaft
  Immortal pow'rs not fubject to the grave.

For though the Soul do feem her grave to bear,
  And in this world is almoft bury'd quick,
We have no caufe the Body's death to fear;
  For when the fhell is broke, out comes a chick.

                              S E C T.

S E C T. XXXIII.

*Three Kinds of Life anſwerable to the three
Powers of the* SOUL.

*F*OR *as* the *Soul's eſſential pow'rs* are three ;
 The *quick'ning pow'r,* the *pow'r of ſenſe* and *reaſon*;
Three kinds of life to her deſigned be,
 Which perfect theſe three pow'rs in their due ſeaſon.

The firſt life in the mother's womb is ſpent,
 Where ſhe the *nurſing pow'r* doth only uſe ;
Where, when ſhe finds defect of nouriſhment,
 Sh' expels her Body, and this world ſhe views.

This we call *birth* ; but if the child could ſpeak,
 He *death* would call it ; and of nature plain,
That ſhe would thruſt him out naked and weak,
 And in his paſſage pinch him with ſuch pain.

Yet out he comes, and in this world is plac'd,
 Where all his *ſenſes* in perfection be ;
Where he finds flow'rs to ſmell, and fruits to taſte,
 And ſounds to hear, and ſundry forms to ſee.

       When

When he hath pafs'd fome time upon the ftage,
  His *reafon* then a little feems to wake;
Which tho' fhe fpring when *fenfe* doth fade with age,
  Yet can fhe here no perfect practice make.

Then doth afpiring *Soul* the Body leave,
  Which we call *death*; but were it known to all,
What *life* our *Souls* do by this *death receive*,
  Men would it *birth*, or *gaol-deliv'ry* call.

In this third life, reafon will be fo bright,
  As that her fpark will like the *fun-beams* fhine,
And fhall of God enjoy the real fight,
  Being ftill increas'd by influence divine.

SECT. XXXVI.

THE CONCLUSION.

O Ignorant poor man! what doft thou bear?
  Lock'd up within the cafket of thy breaft?
What jewels, and what riches haft thou there?
  What heav'nly treafure in fo weak a cheft?

Look

Look in thy *Soul*, and thou fhalt *beauties* find,
   Like thofe which drown'd *Narciffus* in the flood:
Honour and *pleafure* both are in thy mind,
   And all that in the world is counted *good*.

Think of her worth, and think that God did mean,
   This worthy mind fhould worthy things embrace:
Blot not her beauties with thy thoughts unclean,
   Nor her difhonour with thy paffion bafe.

Kill not her *quick'ning pow'r* with furfeitings:
   Mar not her *fenfe* with fenfuality:
Caft not her wit on idle things:
   Make not her *free will* flave to vanity.

And when thou think'ft of her *eternity*,
   Think not that *death* againft her nature is;
Think it a *birth*: and when thou go'ft to die,
   Sing like a fwan, as if thou went'ft to blifs.

And if thou, like a child, didft fear before,
   Being in the dark, where thou didft nothing fee;
Now I have brought thee *torch-light*, fear no more;
   Now when thou dy'ft, thou canft not hood-wink'd
     be.

                       And

And thou my *Soul*, which turn'ft with curious eye,
  To view the beams of thine own form divine,
Know, that thou canft know nothing perfectly,
  While thou art clouded with this flesh of mine.

Take heed of *over-weening*, and compare
  Thy *peacock*'s feet with thy gay *peacock*'s train:
Study the beft and higheft things that are,
  But of thyfelf an humble thought retain.

Caft down thyfelf, and only ftrive to raife
  The glory of thy Maker's facred name:
Ufe all thy pow'rs, that bleffed pow'r to praife,
  Which gives thee pow'r to *be*, and *ufe the fame*.

HYMN

H Y M N S

OF

A S T R E A,

IN

ACROSTICK VERSE.

T H E Beauties of these Acrosticks make some Amends for the innumerable Two-lines of other Writers in this Kind, who are with great Justice ridiculed and condemned by Mr. DRYDEN, *in his* Mac Fleckno ; *and Mr.* ADDISON, *in his* Essay on Wit, *in the First Volume of the Spectators.*

HYMN

HYMN I.

Of Astrea.

E A R L Y before the day doth spring ;
L et us awake my Muse and sing,
I t is no time to slumber,
S o many joys this time doth bring,
A s time will fail to number.

B ut whereunto shall we bend our lays?
E 'en up to Heaven, again to raise
T he Maid which thence descended ;
H ath brought again the golden days,
A nd all the world amended.

R udeness itself she doth refine,
E 'en like an alchymist divine,
G rofs times of iron turning
I nto the purest form of gold ;
N ot to corrupt, till heaven wax old,
A nd be refin'd with burning.

HYMN II.

To Astrea.

ETERNAL Virgin, *Goddess* true,

L et me presume to sing to you.

I ove, e'en great *Jove* hath leisure

S ometimes to hear the vulgar crew,

A nd hears them oft with pleasure.

B lessed *Astrea*, I in part

E njoy the blessings you impart,

T he *peace*, the milk and honey,

H umanity, and civil *art*,

A richer *dow'r* than money.

R ight glad am I that now I live,

E 'en in these days whereto you give

G reat happiness and glory;

I f after you I should be born,

N o doubt I should my birth-day scorn,

A dmiring your sweet story.

HYMN

HYMN III.

To the Spring.

EARTH now is green, and heaven is blue,
L ively spring which makes all new,
I olly spring doth enter ;
S weet young sun-beams do subdue
A ngry, aged winter.

B lasts are mild, and seas are calm,
E very meadow flows with balm,
T he *earth* wears all her riches ;
H armonious birds sing such a psalm,
A s ear and heart bewitches.

R eserve (sweet spring) this nymph of ours,
E ternal garlands of thy flow'rs,
G reen garlands never wasting ;
I n her shall last our *state*'s fair spring,
N ow and for ever flourishing,
A s long as heav'n is lasting.

HYMN IV.

To the Month of May.

E A C H day of thine, sweet month of May,
L ove makes a solemn holy-day.
I will perform like duty,
S ith thou resemblest every way
A strea, queen of beauty.

B oth your fresh beauties do partake,
E ither's aspect doth summer make,
T houghts of young love awaking;
H earts you both do cause to ake,
A nd yet be pleas'd with aching.

R ight dear art thou, and so is she,
E 'en like attracting sympathy,
G ains unto both like dearness;
I ween this made antiquity,
N ame thee, Sweet May of Majesty,
A s being both like in clearness.

HYMN

HYMN V.

To the Lark.

Early chearful mounting lark,
Lights gentle usher, morning's clark;
In merry notes delighting:
Stint awhile thy song and hark,
And learn my new inditing.

Bear up this hymn, to heav'n it bear,
E 'en up to heav'n, and sing it there,
To heav'n each morning bear it;
Have it set to some sweet sphere,
And let the angels hear it.

Renown'd *Astrea*, that great name,
Exceeding great in worth and fame,
Great worth hath so renown'd it,
It is *Astrea*'s name I praise,
Now then, sweet lark, do thou it raise,
And in high heaven resound it.

HYMN

HYMN VI.

To the Nightingale.

Ev'RY night from ev'n to morn,
L ove's chorifter amid the thorn
I s now fo fweet a finger,
S o fweet, as for her fong I fcorn
A pollo's voice and finger.

B ut nightingale, fith you delight
E ver to watch the ftarry night,
T ell all the ftars of heaven,
H eaven never had a ftar fo bright,
A s now to earth is given.

R oyal *Aftrea* makes our day
E ternal with her beams, nor may
G rofs darknefs overcome her ;
I now perceive why fome do write,
N o country hath fo fhort a night,
A s England hath in fummer.

HYMN

HYMN VII.

To the Rose.

E Y E of the garden, queen of flow'rs
L ove's cup wherein lie nectar's pow'rs,
I ngender'd first of nectar :
S weet nurse-child of the spring's young hours,
A nd beauty's fair character.

B left jewel that the earth doth wear,
E 'en when the brave young sun draws near,
T o her hot love pretending ;
H imself likewise like form doth bear,
A t rising and descending.

R ose of the Queen of Love belov'd ;
E ngland's great kings divinely mov'd,
G ave roses in their banner ;
I t shew'd that beauty's rose indeed,
N ow in this age should them succeed,
A nd reign in more sweet manner.

HYMN

H·Y M·N· VIII.

To all the Princes of Europe.

Europe, the earth's sweet paradise :
L et all thy kings that would be wise,
I n *politic devotion,*
S ail hither to observe her eyes,
A nd mark her heavn'ly motion.

B rave princess of this civil age,
E nter into this pilgrimage :
T his saint's tongue's an oracle,
H er eye hath made a prince a page,
A nd works each day a miracle.

R aise but your looks to her, and see
E 'en the true beams of majesty,
G reat princes, mark her duly ;
I f all the world you do survey,
N o forehead spreads so bright a ray,
A nd notes a prince so truly.

HYMN

HYMN. IX.

To Flora.

Empress of flow'rs, tell where away
L ies your sweet court this *May*,
I n *Greenwich* garden alleys:
S ince there the heav'nly pow'rs do play
A nd haunt no other valleys.

B *eauty, virtue, majesty,*
E loquent Muses, three times three,
T he new fresh *hours*, and graces,
H ave pleasure in this place to be,
A bove all other places.

R oses and lillies did them draw,
E re they divine *Astrea* saw,
G ay flow'rs they sought for pleasure :
I nstead of gath'ring crowns of flow'rs,
N ow gather they *Astrea*'s dowers,
A nd bear to heav'n that treasure.

HYMN

HYMN X.

To the Month of September.

Each month hath praise in some degree;
Let May to others seem to be
In sense the sweetest season;
September thou art best to me,
And best doth please my reason.

But neither for thy corn nor wine
Extoll I those mild days of thine,
Though corn and wine might praise thee;
Heav'n gives thee honour more divine;
And higher fortunes raise thee.

Renown'd art thou (sweet Month) for this,
Emong thy days her birth-day is;
Grace, *plenty*, *peace* and *honour*
In one fair hour with her were born,
Now since they still her crown adorn,
And still attend upon her.

HYMN

HYMN XL.

To the Sun.

E YE of the world, fountain of light,
L ife of day, and death of night,
I humbly feek thy kindnefs :
S weet, dazzle not my feeble fight, ;
A nd ftrike me not with blindnefs.

B ehold me mildly from that face,
E 'en where thou now doft run thy race,
T he fphere where now thou turneft ;.
H aving like *Phaeton* chang'd thy place,
A nd yet hearts only burneft.

R ed in her right cheek thou doft rife,
E xalted after in her eyes,
G reat glory there thou fheweft :
I n th' other cheek when thou defcendeft,
N ew rednefs unto it thou lendeft,
A nd fo thy round thou goeft.

HYMN

HYMN XII.

To her Picture.

EXTREME was his audacity,
L ittle his skill that finish'd thee;
I am asham'd and sorry,
S o dull her counterfeit should be,
A nd she so full of glory.

B ut here are colours red and white,
E ach line, and each proportion right;
T hese lines, this red and whiteness,
H ave wanting yet a life and light,
A majesty, and brightness.

R ude counterfeit, I then did err,
E 'en now when I would needs infer
G reat boldness in thy maker:
I did mistake, he was not bold,
N or durst his eyes her eyes behold,
A nd this made him mistake her.

HYMN

HYMN XIII.

Of her Mind.

EARTH, now adieu, my ravifh'd thought
L ifted to heav'n fets thee at naught;
I nfinite is my longing,
S ecrets of angels to be taught,
A nd things to heav'n belonging.

B rought down from heav'n of angels kind,
E v'n now I do admire her *mind*,
T his is my contemplation,
H er clear fweet *fpirit* which is refin'd,
A bove human *creation*.

R ich fun-beam of th' eternal light,
E xcellent *Soul*, how fhall I write;
G ood angels make me able;
I cannot fee but by your eye,
N or, but by your tongue, fignify
A thing fo admirable.

K   HYMN

HYMN XIV.

Of the Sun-beams of her Mind.

EXCEEDING glorious is this star,
L et us behold her beams afar
I n a fide line reflected ;
S ight bears them not, when near they are,
A nd in right lines directed.

B ehold her in her virtue's beams,
E xtending fun-like to all realms ;
T he fun none views too nearly :
H er well of goodnefs in thefe ftreams,
A ppears right well and clearly.

R adiant virtues, if your light
E nfeeble the beft judgment's fight,
G reat fplendor above meafure
I s in the *mind*, from whence you flow :
N o wit may have accefs to know,
A nd view fo bright a treafure.

HYMN

HYMN XV.

Of her Wit.

E YE of that mind moſt quick and clear,

L ike heaven's eye which from his ſphere

I nto all things prieth,

S ees through all things ev'ry where,

A nd all their natures trieth.

B right image of an angel's wit,

E xceeding ſharp and ſwift like it,

T hings inſtantly diſcerning :

H aving a nature infinite,

A nd yet increas'd by learning.

R ebound upon thyſelf thy light,

E njoy thine own ſweet precious ſight

G ive us but ſome reflection ;

I t is enough for us if we,

N ow in her ſpeech, now policy,

A dmire thine high perfection.

HYMN

HYMN XVI.

Of her Will.

E VER well affected *will*,
L oving *goodnefs*, loathing *ill*,
I neftimable treafure!
S ince fuch a power hath power to fpill,
A nd fave us at her pleafure.

B e thou our law, fweet *will*, and fay,
E v'n what thou wilt, we will obey
T his law; if I could read it;
H erein would I fpend night and day,
A nd ftudy ftill to plead it.

R oyal *free-will*, and only *free*,
E ach other will is flave to thee;
G lad is each *will* to ferve thee:
I n thee fuch princely pow'rs is feen,
N o fpirit but takes thee for her queen,
A nd thinks fhe muft obferve thee.

HYMN

HYMN. XVII.

Of her Memory.

EXCELLENT jewels would you fee,
L ovely ladies come with me,
I will (for love I owe you)
S hew you as rich a treafury,
A s Eaft or Weft can fhew you.

B ehold, if you can judge of it,
E v'n that great ftore-houfe of her wit,
T hat beautiful large table,
H er *memory*, wherein is writ
A ll knowledge admirable.

R ead this fair book, and you fhall learn
E xquifite fkill; if you difcern,
G ain heav'n by this difcerning;
I n fuch a memory divine,
N ature did form the Mufes nine,
A nd *Pallas* queen of learning.

HYMN XVIII.

Of her Fancy.

EXQUISITE curiofity,
L ook on thyfelf with judging eye,
I f aught be faulty, leave it :
S o delicate a fantafy
A s this, will ftraight perceive it.

B ecaufe her temper is fo fine,
E ndow'd with harmonies divine ;
T herefore if difcord ftrike it,
H er true proportions do repine,
A nd fadly do miflike it.

R ight otherwife a pleafure fweet,
E 'er fhe takes in actions meet,
G racing with fmiles fuch meetnefs ;
I n her fair forehead beams appear,
N o fummer's day is half fo clear,
A dorn'd with half that fweetnefs.

HYMN

HYMN XIX.

Of the Organs of her Mind.

ECLIPS'D ſhe is, and her bright rays
L y under veils, yet many ways
I s her fair form revealed ;
S he diverſely herſelf conveys,
A nd cannot be concealed.

B y inſtruments her pow'rs appear
E xceedingly well tun'd and clear :
T his lute is ſtill in meaſure,
H olds ſtill in tune, e'en like a ſphere,
A nd yields the world ſweet pleaſure.

R eſolve me, Muſe, how this thing is,
E re a body like to this
G ave heav'n to earthly creature ?
I am but fond this doubt to make
N o doubt the angels bodies take,
A bove our common nature.

HYMN

HYMN XX.

Of the Paſſions of her Heart.

Examine not th' *inſcrutable heart*;
L ight Muſe of her, though ſhe in part
I mpart it to the ſubject ;
S earch not, although from heav'n thou art,
A nd this an heav'nly object.

B ut ſince ſhe hath a heart, we know,
E re ſome paſſions thence do flow,
T hough ever ruled with honour ;
H er judgment reigns, they wait below,
A nd fix their eyes upon her.

R ectify'd ſo, they in their kind
E ncreaſe each virtue of her mind,
G overn'd with mild tranquillity ;
I n all the regions under heav'n,
N o ſtate doth bear itſelf ſo even,
A nd with ſo ſweet facility.

HYMN

HYMN XXI.

Of the innumerable Virtues of her Mind.

E R E thou proceed in these sweet pains
L earn Muse how many drops it rains
I n cold and moist December ;
S um up May flow'rs, and August's grains,
A nd grapes of mild September.

B ear the sea's sand in memory,
E arth's grass, and the stars in sky,
T he little moats which mounted,
H ang in the beams of *Phœbus'* eye;
A nd never can be counted.

R ecount these numbers numberless,
E re thou her virtue can express,
G reat wits this count will cumber.
I nstruct thyself in numb'ring schools ;
N ow courtiers use to beg for fools,
A ll such as cannot number.

HYMN

HYMN XXII.

Of her Wisdom.

E AGLE-ey'd wisdom, life's loadstar,
L ooking near on things afar ;
I ove's best belov'd daughter,
S hows to her spirit all that are,
A s Jove himself hath taught her.

B y this straight rule she rectifies
E ach thought that in her heart doth rise ;
T his is her clear true mirror,
H er *looking-glass*, wherein she spies
A ll forms of truth and error.

R ight princely virtue fit to reign,
E nthroniz'd in her spirit remain,
G uiding our fortunes ever ;
I f we this star once cease to see,
N o doubt our state will shipwreck'd be,
A nd torn and sunk for ever.

HYMN

HYMN XXIII.

Of her Justice.

E XIL'D *Astrea's* come again,
L o here she doth all things maintain
I n *number, weight,* and *measure* :
S he rules us with delightful pain,
A nd we obey with pleasure.

B y *love* she rules more than by *law,*
E 'en her great *mercy* breedeth awe ;
T his is her sword and scepter ;
H erewith she hearts did ever draw,
A nd this guard ever kept her.

R eward doth sit in her right-hand,
E ach virtue thence takes her garland
G ather'd in honour's garden :
I n her left hand (wherein should be
N aught but the sword) sits clemency,
A nd conquers vice with pardon.

HYMN

HYMN XXIV.

Of her Magnanimity.

E v'N as her state, so is her mind,
L ifted above the vulgar kind,
I t treads proud Fortune under;
S un-like it sits above the wind,
A bove the storms and thunder.

B rave spirit, large heart, admiring *nought,*
E steeming each thing as it ought,
T hat swelleth not, nor shrinketh:
H onour is always in her thought,
A nd of great things she thinketh.

R ocks, pillars, and heaven's axle-tree,
E xemplify her constancy;
G reat changes never change her:
I n her sex fears are wont to rise,
N ature permits, virtue denies,
A nd scorns the face of *danger.*

HYMN

HYMN XXV.

Of her Moderation.

EMPRESS of kingdoms though she be,
L arger is her sov'reignty,
I f she herself do govern ;
S ubject unto herself is she,
A nd of herself true sovereign.

B eauty's crown though she do wear,
E xalted into Fortune's chair,
T hron'd like the queen of pleasure :
H er virtues still possess her ear,
A nd counsel her to measure.

R eason, if she incarnate were,
E v'n Reason's self could never bear
G reatness with moderation ;
I 'n her one temper still is seen,
N o liberty claims she as queen,
A nd shews no alteration.

HYMN

HYMN XXVI.

To Envy.

Envy, go weep; my Muſe and I
L augh thee to ſcorn, thy feeble eye
Is dazzled with the glory
S hining in this gay poeſy,
And little golden ſtory.

Behold how my proud quill doth ſhed
E ternal nectar on her head:
The pomp of coronation
H ath not ſuch pow'r her fame to ſpread,
A s this my admiration.

Reſpect my pen as free and frank
E xpecting not reward nor thank,
G reat wonder only moves it;
I never made it mercenary,
N or ſhould my Muſe this burthen carry
A s hir'd but that ſhe loves it.

ORCHES-

ORCHESTRA;

OR, A

POEM

EXPRESSING

The Antiquity and Excellency of
DANCING.

IN A

DIALOGUE

Between PENELOPE and one of her
WOOERS.

NOT FINISHED.

T O

T H E   P R I N C E.

Sir, whatfoever *you* are pleas'd to do,
  It is your fpecial praife, that you are bent,
And fadly fet your princely mind thereto :
  Which makes *you* in each thing fo excellent.

Hence is it, that *you* came fo foon to be
  A man at arms, in ev'ry point aright ;
The faireft flow'r of noble chivalry ;
  And of Saint *George*'s band, the braveft knight.

And hence it is, that all your youthful train
  In aₑivenefs, and grace, *you* do excel,
When you do courtly dancings entertain,
  Then dancing's praife may be prefented well.

To *you*, whofe aₑion adds more praife thereto,
Than all the Mufes with their pens can do.

ORCHESTRA;

OR, A

POEM *on* DANCING.*

1.

WHERE lives the man that never yet did hear
Of chaſte *Penelope, Ulyſſes'* queen ?
Who kept her faith unſpotted twenty year,
  Till he return'd that far away had been,
  And many men, and many towns had ſeen:
    Ten year at ſiege of Troy he ling'ring lay,
    And ten year in the Midland ſea did ſtray.

---

* Sir John Harrington has writ an epigram in commenda-
tion of this poem. See the 2d Book, Epig. 57, at the end of
his Tranſlation of Arioſto's Orlando Furioſo, folio.

It is a great pity, and to be lamented by the poetical world,
that ſo very ingenious a poem ſhould be left unfiniſhed, or what
is more likely, that the imperfect part ſhould be loſt; for in all
probability, he completed it, being written in his youth, in
Queen Elizabeth's reign, as appears from the concluſion.

2.

Homer, to whom the mufes did caroufe
  A great deep cup with heav'nly nectar fill'd,
The greateft, deepeft cup in *Jove*'s great houfe,
  (For *Jove* himfelf had fo exprefsly will'd)
  He drank off all, nor let one drop be fpill'd ;
    Since when, his brain that had before been dry,
    Became the well-fpring of all poetry.

3.

Homer doth tell in his abundant verfe,
  The long laborious travels of the man,
And of his lady too he doth rehearfe,
  How fhe illudes with all the art fhe can,
  Th' ungrateful love which other lords began :
    For of her lord, falfe fame had long fince fworn,
    That *Neptune*'s monfters had his carcafe torn.

4.

All this he tells, but one thing he forgot,
  One thing moft worthy his eternal fong,
But he was old, and blind, and faw it not,
  Or elfe he thought he fhould *Ulyffes* wrong,
  To mingle it his tragic acts among :
    Yet was there not in all the world of things,
    A fweeter burthen for his mufes wings.

5. The

5.

The courtly love *Antinous* did make,
  Antinous that fresh and jolly knight,
Which of the gallants that did undertake
  To win the widow, had most wealth and might,
  Wit to persuade, and beauty to delight.
    The courtly love he made unto the queen,
    Homer forgot as if it had not been.

6.

Sing then *Terpsichore*, my light muse sing
  His gentle art, and *cunning courtesy* :
You lady can remember ev'ry thing,
  For you are daughter of queen memory ;
  But sing a plain and easy melody :
    For the soft mean that warbleth but the ground,
    To my rude ear doth yield the sweetest sound.

7.

One only night's discourse I can report,
  When the great torch-bearer of heav'n was gone
Down in a mask unto the Ocean's court,
  To revel it with *Thetis* all alone ;
  Antinous disguised and unknown,
    Like to the spring in gaudy ornament,
    Unto the castle of the princess went.

The

8.

The fov'reign caftle of the rocky ifle,
  Wherein *Penelope* the princefs lay,
Shone with a thoufand lamps, which did exile
  The fhadows dark, and turn'd the night to day,
    Not *Jove*'s blue tent, what time the funny ray
    Behind the bulwark of the earth retires,
    Is feen to fparkle with more twinkling fires.

9.

That night the Queen came forth from far within,
  And in the prefence of her court was feen ;
For the fweet finger *Phæmius* did begin
  To praife the worthies that at *Troy* had been ;
    Somewhat of her *Ulyffes* fhe did ween.
    In his grave hymn the heav'nly man would fing,
    Or of his wars, or of his wandering.

10.

Pallas that hour with her fweet breath divine
  Infpir'd immortal beauty in her eyes,
That with celeftial glory fhe did fhine,
  Brighter than *Venus* when fhe doth arife
    Out of the waters to adorn the fkies ;
    The wooers all amazed do admire,
    And check their own prefumptuous defire.

11. Only

11.

Only *Antinous* when at firſt he view'd
  Her ſtar-bright eyes that with new honour ſhin'd,
Was not diſmay'd, but therewithal renew'd
  The nobleneſs and ſplendor of his mind ;
  And as he did fit circumſtances find,
    Unto the throne he boldly did advance,
    And with fair manners woo'd the Queen to dance.

12.

" Goddeſs of women, ſith your heav'nlineſs
  " Hath now vouchſaf'd itſelf to repreſent
" To our dim eyes, which tho' they ſee the leſs,
  " Yet are they bleſs'd in their aſtoniſhment,
  " Imitate heaven whoſe beauty's excellent ;
    " Are in continual motion day and night,
    " And move thereby more wonder and delight.

13.

" Let me the mover be, to turn about
  " Thoſe glorious ornaments, that youth and love
" Have fix'd in you, ev'ry part throughout,
  " Which if you will in timely meaſure move,
  " Not all thoſe precious gems in heav'n above
    " Shall yield a ſight more pleaſing to behold,
    " With all their turns and tracings manifold."

L 4   With

14.

With this the modeſt princeſs bluſh'd and ſmil'd
  Like to a clear and roſy eventide ;
And ſoftly did return this anſwer mild :
  " Fair Sir, you needs muſt fairly be deny'd,
  " Where your demand cannot be ſatisfy'd :
    " My feet which only nature taught to go,
    " Did never yet the art of footing know.

15.

" But why perſuade you me to this new rage ?
  " (For all diſorder and miſrule is new.)
" For ſuch miſgovernment in former age
  " Our old divine forefathers never knew ;
  " Who if they liv'd, and did the follies view
    " Which their fond nephews make their chief
      " affairs,
    " Would hate themſelves that had begot ſuch
      " heirs."

16.

" Sole heir of virtue and of beauty both,
  " Whence cometh it (*Antinous* replies)
" That your imperious virtue is ſo loth
  " To grant your beauty her chief exerciſe ?
  " Or from what ſpring doth your opinion riſe.
                " That

" That dancing is a frenzy and a rage,
" Firſt known and us'd in this new fangled age ?

17.

" *Dancing* * (Bright Lady) then began to be,
  " When the firſt ſeeds whereof the world did ſpring,
" The fire, air, earth and water did agree,
  " By love's perſuaſion, nature's mighty king,
  " To leave their firſt diſorder'd combating ;
    " And in a dance ſuch meaſure to obſerve,
    " As all the world their motion ſhould preſerve.

18.

" Since when they ſtill are carried in a round,
  " And changing come one in another's place,
" Yet do they neither mingle nor confound,
  " But ev'ry one doth keep the bounded ſpace
  " Wherein the dance doth bid it turn or trace :
    " This wond'rous miracle did love deviſe,
    " For dancing is love's proper exerciſe.

---

* The antiquity of dancing.

" 19. Like

19.

" Like this, he fram'd the God's eternal bow'r,
  " And of a shapeless and confused mass,
" By his through piercing and digesting pow'r,
  " The turning vault of heaven formed was:
  " Whose starry wheels he hath so made to pass,
    " As that their movings do a music frame,
    " And they themselves still dance unto the same.

20.

" Or if this (all) which round about we see,
  " (As idle *Morpheus* some sick brains have taught)
" Of undivided *motes* compacted be,
  " How was this goodly architecture wrought?
  " Or by what means were they together brought?
    " They err, that say they did concur by chance,
    " Love made them meet in a well order'd dance.

21.

" As when *Amphion* with his charming lyre
  " Begot so sweet a syren of the air,
" That with her rhetoric made the stones conspire
  " The ruin of a city to repair,
  " (A work of wit and reason's wise affair :)
    " So love's smooth tongue, the *motes* such mea-
      " sure taught
    " That they join'd hands, and so the world was
      " wrought.

22. " How

22.

" How juftly then is dancing termed new,
 " Which with the world in point of time begun ;
" Yea time itfelf, (whofe birth *Jove* never knew,
 " And which indeed is elder than the fun)
 " Had not one moment of his age outrun,
  " When out leap'd dancing from the heap of
   " things,
  " And lightly rode upon his nimble wings.

23.

" Reafon hath both her pictures in her treafure,
 " Where *time the meafure of all moving is* ;
" And dancing is a moving all in meafure ;
 " Now if you do refemble that to this,
 " And think both one, I think you think amifs :
  " But if you judge them twins, together got,
  " And time firft born, your judgment erreth not.

24.

" Thus doth it equal age with age enjoy,
 " And yet in lufty youth for ever flow'rs,
" Like love his fire, whom painters make a boy,
 " Yet is he eldeft of the heav'nly pow'rs ;
 " Or like his brother time, whofe winged hours
  " Going and coming will not let him die,
  " But ftill preferve him in his infancy."

25. This

25.

This faid ; the Queen with her fweet lips, divine,
  Gently began to move the fubtle air,
Which gladly yielding, did itfelf incline
  To take a fhape between thofe rubies fair ;
  And being formed, foftly did repair
    With twenty doublings in the empty way,
    Unto *Antinous'* ears, and thus did fay :

26.

" What eye doth fee the heav'n but doth admire
  " When it the movings of the heav'ns doth fee ?
" Myfelf, if I to heav'n may once afpire,
  " If that be dancing, will a dancer be :
  " But as for this your frantic jollity
    " How it began, or whence you did it learn,
    " I never could with reafon's eye difcern."

27.

Antinous anfwer'd : " Jewel of the earth,
  " Worthy you are that heav'nly dance to lead ;
" But for you think our dancing bafe of birth,
  " And newly born but of a brain-fick head,
  " I will forthwith his antique gentry read ;
    " And for I love him, will his herald be,
    " And blaze his arms, and draw his pedigree.

28. " When

28.

" When Love had ſhap'd this world, *this great fair*
 " *wight*,
 " That all wights elſe in this wide womb contains
" And had inſtructed it to dance aright,*
 " A thouſand meaſures with a thouſand ſtrains,
 " Which it ſhould practiſe with delightful pains,
  " Until that fatal inſtant ſhould revolve,
  " When all to nothing ſhould again reſolve.

29.

" The comely order and proportion fair
 " On ev'ry ſide, did pleaſe his wand'ring eye,
" Till glancing thro' the thin tranſparent air,
 " A rude diſorder'd rout he did eſpy
 " Of men and women, that moſt ſpightfully
  " Did one another throng, and croud ſo ſore,
  " That his kind eye in pity wept therefore.

30.

" And ſwifter than the light'ning down he came,
 " Another ſhapeleſs chaos to digeſt,
" He will begin another world to frame,
 " (For Love till all be well will never reſt)
 " Then with ſuch words as cannot be expreſt,

---

* The original of dancing.

" He

" He cuts the troops, that all afunder fling,
" And ere they wift, he cafts them in a ring.

31.

" Then did he rarify the element,
 " And in the centre of the ring appear,
" The beams that from his forehead fpreading went,
 " Begot an horror, and religious fear
 " In all the fouls that round about him were ;
  " Which in their ears attentivenefs procures,
  " While he, with fuch like founds their minds
   " allures.

32.

" How doth confufion's mother, headlong chance,*
 " Put reafon's noble fquadron to the rout ?
" Or how fhould you that have the governance
 " Of nature's children, heav'n and earth throughout,
 " Prefcribe them rules, and live yourfelves without ?
  " Why fhould your fellowfhip a trouble be,
  " Since man's chief pleafure is fociety ?

---

* The fpeech of Love, perfuading men to learn dancing.

33. " If

33.

" If fenfe hath not yet taught you, learn of me
  " A comely moderation and difcreet,
" That your affemblies may well order'd be
  " When my uniting pow'r fhall make you meet,
  " With heav'nly tunes it fhall be temper'd fweet :
    " And be the model of the world's great frame,
    " And you earth's children, *Dancing* fhall it name.

34.

" Behold the *world* how it is *whirled round,*
  " And for it is fo *whirl'd,* is named fo ;
" In whofe large volume many rules are found
  " Of this new art, which it doth fairly fhow :
  " For your quick eyes in wand'ring to and fro
    " From Eaft to Weft, on no one thing can glance,
    " But if you mark it well, it feems to dance.

35.

" Firft you fee *fix'd* in this huge mirror blue
  " Of trembling lights,* a number numberlefs,
" *Fix'd they are* nam'd, but with a name untrue,
  " For they all move, and in a dance exprefs
  " That *great long year* that doth contain no lefs

---

* By the orderly motion of the fixed ftars.

" Than

" Than threefcore hundreds of thofe years in
    " all,
" Which the fun makes with his courfe natural.

36.

" What if to you thefe fparks diforder'd feem
    " As if by chance they had been fcatter'd there ?
" The gods a folemn meafure do it deem,
    " And fee a juft proportion ev'ry where,
    " And know the points whence firft their movings
        " were,
        " To which firft points when all return again,
        " The axle-tree of heav'n fhall break in twain.

37.

" Under that fpangled fky, five wand'ring flames,*
    " Befides the King of Day, and Queen of Night,
" Are wheel'd around, all in their fundry frames,
    " And all in fundry meafures do delight,
    " Yet altogether keep no meafure right :
        " For by itfelf, each doth itfelf advance,
        " And by itfelf, each doth a galliard dance.

---

* Of the planets.

38. *Venus*

38.

Venus, the mother of that baſtard Love,
  " Which doth uſurp the world's great marſhal's
    " name,
" Juſt with the ſun her dainty feet doth move,
  " And unto him doth all the geſtures frame :
  " Now after, now afore, the flatt'ring dame,
    " With divers cunning paſſages doth err,
    " Still him reſpecting that reſpects not her.

39.

" For that brave ſun the father of the day,
  " Doth love this earth, the mother of the night,
" And like a reveller in rich array
  " Doth dance his galliard in his leman's ſight
  " Both back, and forth, and ſideways paſſing light,
    " His princely grace doth ſo the gods amaze,
    " That all ſtand ſtill and at his beauty gaze.

40.

" But ſee the earth, when he approacheth near,
  " How ſhe for joy doth ſpring, and ſweetly ſmile ;
" But ſee again her ſad and heavy cheer
  " When changing places he retires a while :
  " But thoſe black clouds he ſhortly will exile,
    " And make them all before his preſence fly,
    " As miſts conſum'd before his chearful eye.

M   41. " Who

41.

" Who doth not fee the meafures of the moon,
　" Which thirteen times fhe danceth ev'ry year ?
 " And ends her pavin, thirteen times as foon
　" As doth her brother, of whofe golden hair
　" She borroweth part and proudly doth it wear :
　　" Then doth fhe coily turn her face afide,
　　" That half her cheek is fcarce fometimes defcry'd.

42.

" Next her, the pure, fubtle, and cleanfing fire *
　" Is fwiftly carried in a circle even :
" Though *Vulcan* be pronounc'd by many a liar
　" The only halting god that dwells in heav'n :
　" But that foul name may be more fitly giv'n
　　" To your falfe fire, that far from heav'n is fall,
　　" And doth confume, wafte, fpoil, diforder all.

43.

" And now behold your tender nurfe the *air*, †
　" And common neighbour that *aye runs around*,
" How many pictures and impreffions fair
　" Within her empty regions are there found,
　" Which to your fenfes dancing do propound ;

---

* Of the fire.　　† Of the air.

" For

" For what are *breath, speech, echoes, music, winds,*
" But dancings of the air in sundry kinds ?

44.

" For when you breathe, the *air* in order moves,
   " Now in, now out, in time and measure true ;
" And when you speak, so well she dancing loves,
   " That doubling oft, and oft redoubling new,
   " With thousand forms she doth herself endue :
      " For all the words that from your lips repair,
      " Are naught but tricks and turnings of the air.

45.

" Hence is her prattling daughter *echo* born,
   " That dances to all voices she can hear :
" There is no sound so harsh that she doth scorn,
   " Nor any time wherein she will forbear
   " The airy pavement with her feet to wear :
      " And yet her hearing sense is nothing quick,
      " For after time she endeth ev'ry trick.

46.

" And thou sweet *music*, dancing's only life,
   " The ear's sole happiness, the air's best speech,
" Loadstone of fellowship, charming rod of strife,
   " The soft mind's paradise, the sick mind's leech,
   " With thine own tongue thou trees and stones can
      " teach,

M 2   " That

" " That when the air doth dance her fineſt mea-
" " ſure,
" " Then art thou born the gods and mens ſweet
" " pleaſure.

47.

" Laſtly, where keep the *winds* their revelry,
" " Their violent turnings, and wild whirling hays?
" But in the air's tranſlucent gallery?
" " Where ſhe herſelf is turn'd a hundred ways,
" " While with thoſe maſkers wantonly ſhe plays;
" " Yet in this miſrule, they ſuch rule embrace,
" " As two at once encumber not the place.

48.

" If then fire, air, wand'ring and fix'd lights
" " In ev'ry province of the imperial ſky,
" Yield perfect forms of dancing to your ſights,
" " In vain I teach the ear, that which the eye
" " With certain view already doth deſcry.
" " But for your eyes perceive not all they ſee,
" " In this I will your ſenſes maſter be.

49. " For

49.

" For lo the *sea** that fleets about the land,
  " And like a girdle clips her folid waift,
" Mufic and meafure both doth underftand :
  " For his great chryftal eye is always caft
  " Up to the moon, and on her fixed faft :
    " And as fhe danceth in her pallid fphere,
    " So danceth he about the centre here.

50.

" Sometimes his proud green waves in order fet,
  " One after other flow unto the fhore,
" Which when they have with many kiffes wet,
  " They ebb away in order as before ;
  " And to make known his courtly love the more,
    " He oft doth lay afide his three-fork'd mace,
    " And with his arms the tim'rous earth embrace.

51.

" Only the earth doth ftand for ever ftill,
  " Her rocks remove not, nor her mountains meet,
" (Although fome wits enrich'd with learning's fkill
  " Say heav'n ftands firm, and that the earth doth fleet,
  " And fwiftly turneth underneath their feet)

---

* Of the fea.

" Yet

" Yet though the earth is ever ſtedfaſt ſeen,
" On her broad breaſt hath dancing ever been.

52.

" For thoſe blue veins that through her body ſpread,
  " Thoſe ſapphire ſtreams which from great hills do
    " ſpring,*
" (The earth's great dugs ; for ev'ry wight is fed
  " With ſweet freſh moiſture from them iſſuing)
  " Obſerve a dance in their wild wand'ring :
    " And ſtill their dance begets a murmur ſweet,
    " And ſtill the murmur with the dance doth
      " meet.

53.

" Of all their ways I love meander's path,
  " Which to the tune of dying ſwans doth dance,
" Such winding flights, ſuch turns and cricks he hath,
  " Such creaks, ſuch wrenches and ſuch dalliance ;
  " That whether it be hap or heedleſs chance,
    " In this indented courſe and wriggling play
    " He ſeems to dance a perfect cunning hay.

---

* Of the rivers.

54. " But

54.

" But wherefore do thefe ftreams for ever run ?
  " To keep themfelves for ever fweet and clear :
" For let their everlafting courfe be done,
  " They ftraight corrupt and foul with mud appear.
  " O ye fweet nymphs that beauty's lofs do fear,
    " Contemn the drugs that phyfic doth devife,
    " And learn of love this dainty exercife.

55.

" See how thofe flow'rs that have fweet beauty too,
  " (The only jewels that the earth doth wear, *
" When the young fun in bravery her doth woo)
  " As oft as they the whiftling wind do hear,
  " Do wave their tender bodies here and there ;
    " And tho' their dance no perfect meafure is,
    " Yet oftentimes their mufic makes them kifs.

56.

" What makes the vine about the elm to dance,
  " With turnings, windings, and embracements
    " round ?
" What makes the loadftone to the north advance
  " His fubtle point, as if from thence he found
  " His chief attracting virtue to redound ?

---

* Of other things upon the earth.

                  " Kind

" Kind nature first doth cause all things to love,
" Love makes them dance and in just order move.

57.

" Hark how the birds do sing, and mark then how
    " Jump with the modulation of their lays,
" They lightly leap, and skip from bough to bough ;
    " Yet do the cranes deserve a greater praise
    " Which keep such measure in their airy ways,
        " As when they all in order ranked are,
        " They make a perfect form triangular.

58.

" In the chief angle flies the watchful guide,
    " And all the followers their heads do lay
" On their foregoers backs, on either side ;
    " But for the captain hath no rest to stay
    " His head forwearied with the windy way,
        " He back retires, and then the next behind,
        " As his lieutenant leads them thro' the wind.

59.

" But why relate I ev'ry singular ?
    " Since all the world's great fortunes and affairs
" Forward and backward rapp'd and whirled are,
    " According to the music of the spheres :
    " And change herself, her nimble feet upbears

                                        " On

" On a round flippery wheel that rolleth ay,
" And turns all ftates with her imperious fway.

60.

" Learn then to dance, you that are princes born,
" And lawful lords of earthly creatures all ;
" Imitate them, and therefore take no fcorn,
" For this new art to them is natural
" And imitate the ftars celeftial :
" For when pale death your vital twift fhall fever,
" Your better parts muft dance with them for
" ever.

61.

" Thus Love perfuades, and all the crowd of men
" That ftands around doth make a murmuring :
" As when the wind loos'd from his hollow den,
" Among the trees a gentle bafe doth fing,
" Or as a brook through pebbles wandering :
" But in their looks they utter'd this plain fpeech,
" That they would learn to dance, if Love would
" teach.*

---

* How Love taught men to dance.

" Then

62.

" Then firſt of all he doth demonſtrate plain
  " The motions ſeven that are in nature found,
" Upward and downward, forth, and back again,
  " To this ſide, and to that, and turning round; *
  " Whereof a thouſand brawls he doth compound,
    " Which he doth teach unto the multitude,
    " And ever with a turn they muſt conclude.

63.

" As when a nymph ariſing from the land,
  " Leadeth a dance with her long watery train
" Down to the ſea, ſhe wryes to every hand,
  " And every way doth croſs the fertile plain :
  " But when at laſt ſhe falls into the main,
    " Then all her traverſes concluded are,
    " And with the ſea, her courſe is circular.

64.

" Thus when at firſt Love had them marſhalled,
  " As erſt he did the ſhapeleſs maſs of things,
" He taught them rounds and winding hays to tread,
  " And about trees to caſt themſelves in rings :
  " As the two Bears, whom the firſt mover flings

---

* Rounds or Country Dances.

" With

" With a fhort turn about heaven's axle-tree,
" In a round dance for ever wheeling be.

65.

" But after thefe, as men more civil grew,
  " He did more grave and f lemn meafures frame,*
" With fuch fair order and proportion true,
  " And correfpondence ev'ry way the fame,
  " That no fault-finding eye did ever blame.
    " For ev'ry eye was moved at the fight
    " With fober wond'ring, and with fweet delight.

66.

" Not thofe young ftudents of the heav'nly book,
  " *Atlas* the great, *Prometheus* the wife,
" Which on the ftars did all their life-time look,
  " Could ever find fuch meafure in the fkies,
  " So full of change and rare varieties ;
    " Yet all the feet whereon thefe meafures go,
    " Are only fpondees, folemn, grave and flow.

---

* Me.fures.

67. " But

67.

" But for more diverfe and more pleafing fhow,
  " A fwift and wand'ring dance * fhe did invent,
" With paffages uncertain to and fro,
  " Yet with a certain anfwer and confent
  " To the quick mufic of the inftrument.
    " Five was the number of the mufic's feet,
    " Which ftill the dance did with five paces meet.

68.

" A gallant dance, that lively doth bewray
  " A fpirit and a virtue mafculine,
" Impatient that her houfe on earth fhou'd ftay
  " Since fhe herfelf is fiery and divine :
  " Oft doth fhe make her body upward fine ;
    " With lofty turns and capriols in the air,
    " Which with the lufty tunes accordeth fair.

69.

" What fhall I name thofe current traverfes, †
  " That on a triple dactyl foot do run
" Clofe by the ground with fliding paffages,
  " Wherein that dancer greateft praife hath won
  " Which with beft order can all orders fhun :

---

      * Galliards.   † Courantoes.

                                " For

" For ev'ry where he wantonly muſt range,
" And turn, and wind, with unexpected change.

70.

" Yet is there one the moſt delightful kind,
  " A lofty jumping, or a leaping round, *
" Where arm in arm, two dancers are entwin'd,
  " And whirl themſelves with ſtrict embracements
    " bound,
  " And ſtill their feet an *anapeſt* do ſound :
    " An *anapeſt* is all their muſic's ſong,
    " Whoſe firſt two feet are ſhort, and third is long.

71.

" As the victorious twins of *Leda* and *Jove*
  " That taught the *Spartans* dancing on the ſands,
" Of ſwift *Eurotas*, dance in heav'n above,
  " Knit and united with eternal hands ;
  " Among the ſtars their double image ſtands,
    " Where both are carried with an equal pace,
    " Together jumping in their turning race.

---

* Lavoltaes.

72. " This

72.

" This is the net wherein the fun's bright eye
   " *Venus* and *Mars* entangled did behold,
" For in this dance, their arms they so employ,
   " As each doth feem the other to enfold :
   " What if lewd wits another tale have told
      " Of jealous *Vulcan*, and of iron chains ?
      " Yet this true fenfe that forged lie contains.

73.

" Thefe various forms of dancing, Love did frame,
   " And befide thefe, a hundred millions more,
" And as he did invent, he taught the fame,
   " With goodly gefture, and with comely fhow,
   " Now keeping ftate, now humbly honouring low :
     " And ever for the perfons and the place
     " He taught moft fit, and beft accordin g grac*

74.

" For Love, within his fertile working brain
   " Did then conceive thofe gracious virgins three,
" Whofe civil moderation does maintain
   " All decent order and conveniency,
   " And fair refpect, and feemly modefty :

---

* Grace in dancing.

                           " And

" And then he thought it fit they fhould be
" born,
" That their fweet prefence dancing might
" adorn.

75.

" Hence is it that thefe Graces painted are
" With hand in hand dancing an endlefs round:
" And with regarding eyes, that ftill beware
" That there be no difgrace amongft them found;
" With equal foot they beat the flow'ry ground,
" Laughing, or finging, as their paffions will,
" Yet nothing that they do becomes them ill.

76.

" Thus Love taught men, and men thus learn'd of
" Love
" Sweet mufic's found with feet to counterfeit,
" Which was long time before high thund'ring
" *Jove*
" Was lifted up to heaven's imperial feat:
" For though by birth he were the prince of
" *Crete,*
" Nor *Crete,* nor heav'n, fhould the young
" prince have feen
" If dancers with their timbrels had not been.

33. " Since

77.

" Since when all ceremonious myfteries,
  " All facred orgies and religious rights,
" All pomps, and triumphs, and folemnities,
  " All funerals, nuptials, and like public fights,
  " All parliaments of peace, and warlike fights,
   " All learned arts, and every great affair
   " A lively fhape of dancing feems to bear. *

78.

" For what did he who with his ten-tongu'd lute
  " Gave beafts and blocks an underftanding ear ?
" Or rather into beftial minds and brute
  " Shed and infus'd the beams of reafon clear ?
  " Doubtlefs for men that rude and favage were
   " A civil form of dancing he devis'd,
   " Wherewith unto their gods they facrific'd.

79.

" So did *Mufæus*, fo *Amphion* did,
  " And *Linus* with his fweet enchanting fong,
" And he whofe hand the earth of monfters rid,
  " And had men's ears faft chained to his tongue :
  " And *Thefeus* to his wood-born flaves among,

---

* The ufe and forms of dancing in fundry affairs of man's life.

                            " Us'd

" Us'd dancing as the fineſt policy
" To plant religion and ſociety.

80.

" And therefore now the Thracian *Orpheus'* lyre
" And *Hercules* himſelf are ſtellify'd;
" And in high heaven amidſt the ſtarry quire
" Dancing their parts continually do ſide:
" So on the zodiac *Garymede* doth ride,
" And ſo is *Hebe* with the muſes nine
" For pleaſing *Jove* with dancing, made divine.

81.

" Wherefore was *Proteus* ſaid himſelf to change
" Into a ſtream, a lion, and a tree,
" And many other forms fantaſtic ſtrange,
" As in his fickle thought he wiſh'd to be?
" But that he danc'd with ſuch facility,
" As like a lion he could pace with pride,
" Ply like a plant, and like a river ſide.

82.

" And how was *Cæneus* made at firſt a man,
" And then a woman, then a man again
" But in a dance? which when he firſt began
" He the man's part in meaſure did ſuſtain:
" But when he chang'd into a ſecond ſtrain,

N

" He

" He danc'd the woman's part another space,
" And then return'd into his former place.

83.

" Hence sprang the fable of *Tiresias*,
  " That he the pleasure of both sexes try'd :
" For in a dance he man and woman was
  " By often change of place from side to side :
  " But for the woman easily did slide,
    " And smoothly swim with cunning hidden art,
" He took more pleasure in a woman's part.

84.

" So to a fish *Venus* herself did change,
  " And swimming thro' the soft and yielding wave,
" With gentle motions did so smoothly range
  " As none might see where she the water drave :
  " But this plain truth that falsed fable gave,
    " That she did dance with sliding easiness,
    " Pliant and quick in wand'ring passages.

85.

" And merry *Bacchus* practis'd dancing too,
  " And to the Lydian numbers rounds did make :
" The like he did in th' Eastern India do,
  " And taught them all when *Phœbus* did awake,
  " And when at night he did his coach forsake,

" To

" To honour heav'n, and heav'ns great rolling eye
" With turning dances, and with melody.

86.

" Thus they who firft did found a common-weal,
" And they who firft religion did ordain,
" By dancing firft the people's hearts did fteal,
" Of whom we now a thoufand tales do feign ;
" Yet do we now their perfect rules retain,
" And ufe them ftill in fuch devifes new,
" As in the world long fince their withering grew.

87.

" For after towns and kingdoms founded were,
" Between great ftates arofe well-ordered *war* ;
" Wherein moft perfect meafure doth appear,
" Whether their well-fet ranks refpected are
" In quadrant form or femicircular :
" Or elfe the march, when all the troops advance,
" And to the drum in gallant order dauce.

88.

" And after wars, when white-wing'd victory
" Is with a glorious triumph beautify'd,
" And ev'ry one doth *Iō Iō* cry,
" Whilft all in gold the conquerer doth ride ;
" The folemn pomp that fills the city wide

N 2   " Obferves

" Obferves fuch rank and meafure every where,
" As if they altogether dancing were.

89.

" The like juft order mourners do obferve,
(" But with unlike affection and attire)
" When fome great man that nobly did deferve,
" And whom his friends impatiently defire,
" Is brought with honour to his lateft fire :
" The dead corpfe too in that fad dance is mov'd,
" As if both dead and living dancing lov'd.

90.

" A diverfe caufe, but like folemnity
" Unto the temple leads the bafhful bride,
" Which blufheth like the Indian ivory
" Which is with dip of Tyrian purple dy'd :
" A golden troop doth pafs on ev'ry fide
" Of flourifhing young men and virgins gay,
" Which keep fair meafure all the flow'ry way.

91.

" And not alone the general multitude,
" But thofe choice *Neftors* which in council grave
" Of cities, and of kingdoms do conclude,
" Moft comely order in their feffions have :
" Wherefore the wife Theffalians ever gave

" The

" The name of leader of their countries dance
" To him that had their countries governance.

92.

" And those great masters of their liberal arts
" In all their several schools do dancing teach,
" For humble grammar first doth set the parts
" Of congruent and well-according speech :
" Which rhetoric whose state the clouds doth reach,
" And heav'nly poetry do forward lead,
" And divers measure diversely do tread.

93.

" For rhetoric clothing speech in rich array
" In looser numbers teacheth her to range,
" With twenty tropes, and turnings ev'ry way,
" And various figures, and licentious change ;
" But poetry with rule and order strange
" So curiously doth move each single pace,
" As all is mar'd if she one foot misplace.

94.

" These arts of speech the guides and marshals are ;
" But logic leadeth reason in a dance,
" Reason the connoisseur and bright load-star,
" In this world's sea t' avoid the rock of chance,
" For with close following and continuance

N 3   " One

" One reafon doth another fo enfue,
" As in conclufion ftill the dance is true.

95.

" So mufic to her own fweet tunes doth trip
" With tricks of, 3, 5, 8, 15, and more :
" So doth the art of numb'ring feem to fkip
" From even to odd in her proportion'd fcore :
" So do thofe fkills, whofe quick eyes do explore
" The juft dimenfion both of earth and heaven,
" In all their rules obferve a meafure even.

96.

" Lo this is dancing's true nobility :
" Dancing the child of mufic and of love ;
" Dancing itfelf both love and harmony,
" Where all agree, and all in order move ;
" Dancing the art that all arts do approve :
" The fair character of the world's confent,
" The heav'ns true figure, and th' earth's orna-
" ment."

97.

The queen, whofe dainty ears had borne too long
The tedious praife of that fhe did defpife,
Adding once more the mufic of the tongue
To the fweet fpeech of her alluring eyes,
Began to anfwer in fuch winning wife,

As

As that forthwith *Antinous'* tongue was ty'd,
His eyes faft fix'd, his ears were open wide.

98.

" Forfooth (quoth fhe) great glory you have won,
  " To your trim minion dancing all this while,
" By blazing him Love's firft begotten fon;
  " Of ev'ry ill the hateful father vile
  " That doth the world with forceries beguile :
    " Cunningly mad, religioufly prophane,
    " Wit's monfter, reafon's canker, fenfe's bane.

99.

" Love taught the mother that unkind defire
  " To wafh her hands in her own infant's blood ;
" Love taught the daughter to betray her fire
  " Into moft bafe and worthy fervitude ;
  " Love taught the brother to prepare fuch food
    " To feaft his brother, that the all-feeing fun
    " Wrapt in a cloud, that wicked fight did fhun.

100.

" And ev'n this felf fame Love hath dancing taught,
  " An art that fheweth th' *idea* of his mind
" With vainnefs, frenzy, and miforder fraught ;
  " Sometimes with blood and cruelties unkind :
  " For in a dance, *Tereus* mad wife did find

" Fit

" Fit time and place by murder of her fon,
" T' avenge the wrong his traiterous fire had
" done.

101.

" What mean the mermaids when they dance and fing
" But certain death unto the mariner ?
" What tidings do the dancing dolphins bring,
" But that fome dangerous ftorm approacheth near ?
" Then fith both love and dancing liveries bear
" Of fuch ill hap, unhappy may I prove,
" If fitting free I either dance or love."

102.

Yet once again *Antinous* did reply ;
" Great Queen, condemn not Love * the innocent,
" For this mifchevious luft, which traiteroufly
" Ufurps his name, and fteals his ornament :
" For that true love which dancing did invent,
" Is he that tun'd the world's whole harmony,
" And link'd all men in fweet fociety.

---

* True Love inventor of dancing.

103. " He

103.

" He firſt extracted from th' earth-mingled mind
  " That heav'nly fire, or quinteſſence divine,
" Which doth ſuch ſympathy in beauty find,
    " As is between the elm and fruitful vine,
    " And ſo to beauty ever doth incline :
      " Life's life it is, and cordial to the heart,
      " And of our better part, the better part.

104.

" This _is true Love_, by that true _Cupid_ got,
    " Which danceth galliards in your am'rous eyes,
" But to your frozen heart approacheth not,
    " Only your heart he dares not enterprize ;
    " And yet thro' every other part he flies,
      " And every where he nimbly danceth now,
      " That in yourſelf, yourſelf perceive not how.

105.

" For your ſweet beauty daintily transfus'd
    " With due proportion throughout ev'ry part,
" What is it but a dance where Love hath us'd
    " His finer cunning, and more curious art ;
    " Where all the elements themſelves impart,
      " And turn, and wind, and mingle with ſuch
        " meaſure,
      " That th' eye that ſees it, ſurfeits with the
        " pleaſure ?

                                      " Love

106.

" Love in the twinkling of your eyelids danceth,
 " Love danceth in your pulfes and your veins,
" Love when you fow, your needles point advanceth,.
  " And makes it dance a thoufand curious ftrains
  " Of winding rounds, whereof the form remains :
    " To fhew, that your fair hands can dance the
      " hay,
    " Which your fine feet would learn as well as
      " they.

107.

" And when your ivory fingers touch the ftrings
  " Of any filver-founding inftrument,
" Love makes them dance to thofe fweet murmur-
    " ings,
  " With bufy fkill, and cunning excellent :
  " O that your feet thofe tunes would reprefent
    " With artificial motions to and fro,
    " That Love this art in ev'ry part might fhow !

108.

" Yet your fair foul, which came from heav'n above
  " To rule this houfe, another heav'n below,
" With divers powers in harmony doth move,
    " And all the virtues that from her do flow,
    " In a round meafure hand in hand do go :
      " Could I now fee, as I conceive this dance,
      " Wonder and love would caft me in a trance.

109. " The

109.

" The richeſt jewel in all the heav'nly treaſure
  " That ever yet unto the earth was ſhown,
" Is perfect concord, th' only perfect pleaſure
  " That wretched earth-born men have ever known,
  " For many hearts it doth compound in one :
    " That what ſo one doth will, or ſpeak, or do,
    " With one conſent they all agree thereto,

110.

" Concord's true picture ſhineth in this art,
  " Where divers men and women ranked be,
" And every one doth dance a ſeveral part,
  " Yet all as one, in meaſure do agree,
  " Obſerving perfect uniformity :
    " All turn together, all together trace,
    " And all together honour and embrace.

111.

" If they whom ſacred love hath link'd in one,
  " Do, as they dance, in all their courſe of life ;
" Never ſhall burning grief nor bitter moan,
  " Nor factious difference, nor unkind ſtrife,
  " Ariſe betwixt the huſband and the wife :
    " For whether forth or back, or round he go,
    " As the man doth, ſo muſt the woman do.

111. " What

112.

" What if by often interchange of place
 " Sometime the woman gets the upper hand?
" That is but done for more delightful grace,
 " For on that part she doth not ever stand:
 " But, as the measure's law doth her command,
 " She wheels about, and ere the dance doth end,
 " Into her former place she doth tranfcend.

113.

" But not alone this correfpondence meet
 " And uniform confent doth dancing praife,
" For comelinefs the child of order fweet
 " Enamels it with her eye-pleafing rays:
 " Fair comelinefs, ten hundred thoufand ways,
 " Thro' dancing fheds itfelf, and makes it fhine,
 " With glorious beauty, and with grace divine.

114.

" For comelinefs is a difpofing fair
 " Of things and actions in fit time and place;
" Which doth in dancing fhew itfelf moft clear,
 " When troops confus'd, which here and there do
 " trace
 " Without diftinguifhment or bounded fpace,
 " By dancing rule into fuch ranks are brought,
 " As glads the eye, as raviflieth the thought.

                                   115. " Then

115.

" Then why fhould reafon judge that reafonlefs
" Which is wit's offspring, and the work of art,
" Image of concord and of comelinefs.
" Who fees a clock moving in every part,
" A failing pinnace, or a wheeling cart,
" But thinks that reafon, ere it came to pafs,
" The firft impulfive caufe and mover was ?

116.

" Who fees an army all in rank advance,
" But deems a wife commander is in place
" Which leadeth on that brave victorious dance ?
" Much more in dancing's art, in dancing's grace
" Blindnefs itfelf may reafon's footfteps trace :
" *For of Love's maze it is the curious plot*
" *And of mans fellowfhip the true-love knot.*

117.

" But if thefe eyes of yours, (load-ftars of love
" Shewing the world's great dance to your minds
" eye)
" Cannot with all their demonftrations move
" Kind apprehenfion in your fantafy
" Of dancing's virtue, and nobility :
" How can my barbarous tongue win you thereto,
" Which heav'n and earth's fair fpeech could
" never do ?

118. " O Love

118.

" O Love my king; if all my wit and power
  " Have done you all the fervice that they can,
" O be you prefent in this prefent hour,
  " And help your fervant and your true liege-man,
  " End that perfuafion which I erft began :
    " For who in praife of dancing can perfuade
    " With fuch fweet force as Love, which dancing
      " made ?"

119.

Love heard his pray'r, and fwifter than the wind
  Like to a page, in habit, face, and fpeech,
He came, and ftood *Antinous* behind,*
  And many fecrets to his thoughts did teach :
  At laft a chryftal mirror he did reach
    Unto his hands, that he with one rafh view,
    All forms therein by Love's revealing knew.

120.

And humbly honouring, gave it to the queen
  With this fair fpeech : " See faireft queen (quoth he)
" The faireft fight that ever fhall be feen,
  " And th' only wonder of pofterity,
  " The richeft work in nature's treafury;

---

* A paffage to the defcription of dancing in that age.

" Which

" Which she disdains to shew on this world's stage,
" And thinks it far too good for our rude age.

121.

" But in another world divided far,
" In the great, fortunate triangled isle,
" Thrice twelve degrees remov'd from the north star,
" She will this glorious workmanship compile,
" Which she hath been conceiving all this while
" Since the world's birth, and will bring forth
" at last,
" When six and twenty hundred years are past.".

122.

Penelope, the queen, when she had view'd
The strange eye-dazzling admirable light,
Fain would have prais'd the state and pulchritude,
But she was stricken dumb with wonder quite,
Yet her sweet mind retain'd her thinking might:
Her ravish'd mind in heav'nly thoughts did dwell,
But what she thought, no mortal tongue can tell.

123.

You lady muse, whom Jove the counsellor
Begot of memory, wisdom's treasuress,
To your divining tongue is given a power
Of uttering secrets large and limitless:
You can Penelope's strange thoughts express

Which

Which fhe conceiv'd, and then would fain have
 told,
When fhe the wond'rous chryftal did behold.

124.

Her winged thoughts bore up her mind fo high,
 As that fhe ween'd fhe faw the glorious throne
Where the bright moon doth fit in majefty,
 A thoufand fparkling ftars about her fhone;
 But fhe herfelf did fparkle more alone
  Than all thofe thoufand beauties would have done
  If they had been confounded all in one.

125.

And yet fhe thought thofe ftars mov'd in fuch meafure,
 To do their fovereign honour and delight,
As footh'd her mind with fweet enchanting pleafure,
 Although the various change amaz'd her fight,
 And her weak judgment did entangle quite :
  Befide, their moving made them fhine more clear,
  As diamonds mov'd, more fparkling do appear.

126.

This was the picture of her wondrous thought ;
 But who can wonder that her thought was fo,
Sith *Vulcan* king of fire that mirrour wrought,
 (Who things to come, prefent, and paft, doth know)
 And there did reprefent in lively fhow
        Our

Our glorious Englifh court's divine image,
As it fhould be in this our golden age ?

Here are wanting fome Stanzas defcribing
QUEEN ELIZABETH.

Then follow thefe.

127.

Her brighter dazzling beams of majefty
  Were laid afide, for fhe vouchfaf'd awhile
With gracious, chearful, and familiar eye
  Upon the revels of her court to fmile ;
  For fo time's journies fhe doth oft beguile :
    Like fight no mortal eye might elfewhere fee
    So full of ftate, art, and variety.

128.

For of her barons brave, and ladies fair,
 (Who had they been elfewhere moft fair had been)
Many an incomparable lovely pair,
 With hand in hand were interlinked feen,
 Making fair honour to their fovereign queen;
  Forward they pac'd, and did their pace apply
  To a moft fweet and folemn melody.

129.

So fubtile and fo curious was the meafure,
 With unlook'd for change in ev'ry ftrain;
As that *Penelope* wrapt with fweet pleafure,
 When fhe beheld the true proportion plain
 Of her own web, weav'd and unweav'd again;
  But that her art was fomewhat lefs fhe thought,
  And on a meer ignoble fubject wrought.

130.

For here, like to the filkworm's induftry,
 Beauty itfelf out of itfelf did weave
So rare a work, and of fuch fubtlety,
 As did all eyes entangle and deceive,
 And in all minds a ftrange impreffion leave:
  In this fweet labyrinth did *Cupid* ftray,
  And never had the power to pafs away.

131. As

131.

As when the Indians, neighbours of the morning,
  In honour of the chearful rifing fun,
With pearl and painted plumes themfelves adorning,
  A folemn ftately meafure have begun ;
  The god, well pleas'd with that fair honour done,
    Sheds forth his beams, and doth their faces kifs
    With that immortal glorious face of his.

132.

So &c. &c.   &   &   &   &

F I N I S.

E R R A T A.

In the Note Page i of the Introduction, inftead of the Letters *W. B.* at the End of it, read *W. T.* In the Poem on
the Immortality of the Soul Page 101, iftead of S E C T.
XXXVI. read S E C T. XXXIV. In the Note facing the
Hymns of Aftrea Page 107, inftead of *Two-lines* read *Foderies.*